PRAISE FOR *THE BOY IN THE FIELD*

"In the broadest sense, Margot Livesey's exquisite novel *The Boy in the Field* is a whodunit. . . . But the real mysteries lie elsewhere, specifically and most compellingly with the characters who are witnesses to the crime. . . . Livesey's writing is quiet, observant, and beautifully efficient—there's not an extra word or scene in the entire book—and yet simultaneously so cinematic, you can hear the orchestral soundtrack as you tear through the pages." —*New York Times Book Review*

"An expertly crafted novel of family (and one almost magically good dog) filled with dazzling insights and beauty."
—*People*, Book of the Week

"Margot Livesey is a literary pointillist whose prose is both impressionistic and as precise as a geometry equation. . . . Tiny piece by tiny piece, Livesey builds an intimate universe that expands and expands until it grows large enough, almost, to keep everything else at bay." —*O, the Oprah Magazine*

"Written in elegant, spare prose, this story flies swiftly forward from the transfixing opening pages. A charming, complicated family dynamic, a twist of eerie magic."
—Tessa Hadley, author of *Late in the Day*

"Luminous. . . . Livesey's language is crystalline-clear and immersive. . . . Ultimately what keeps Livesey's novel aloft is that it is full of kindnesses . . . as well as Livesey's precisely evocative words. At one point, Duncan tears a handful of his sketches in half, 'enjoying the decisive sound of fibers parting.' Like so many other moments in this novel, that description nails the moment, the character, and the elemental aspect of the book in one fell, satisfactory swoop." —*Boston Globe*

"A swift-moving mystery that expands into subtler sorts of narratives—the coming of age, the family in crisis—Margot Livesey's ninth novel, *The Boy in the Field*, once more demonstrates how she's the best sort of pro."
—*Minneapolis Star Tribune*

"From its taut and frightening opening chapter to its final, mournful pages, *The Boy in the Field* is a tender, deeply humane exploration of family, philosophy, and what it means to grow up, to keep secrets, to care for one another, and, most importantly, what it means to hold another's heart in yours, always, with tenderness and mercy."
—Elizabeth Wetmore, author of *Valentine*

"This is fiction at its fullest. . . . In this novel, dazzling, shifting points of views and possibilities reveal more than the expected mysteries." —Michael Silverblatt, *Bookworm*

"Margot Livesey has the unique ability to find the hidden darkness beneath the surface of our lives, no matter how deeply buried. A deceptively simple story that explores the aftermath of a moment of violence, *The Boy in the Field* amazed me with its insight and the subtlety of Livesey's beautiful, almost dreamlike prose. She speaks of a sensation—'quick as a mousetrap, sharp as a thorn'—and I can't think of a better description of her work. Quick and sharp."

—Kevin Wilson, author of *Nothing to See Here*

"Powerfully affecting."   —*Kirkus Reviews*, starred review

"Every character rings true; every observation and reaction feels real. Braiding three separate views of the same incident, Livesey weaves a masterful tapestry of emotion and action focused on the indelible impact of random events."

—*Booklist*, starred review

"I loved every single sentence of *The Boy in the Field*. This novel is so intricately woven, its world so vibrantly built, its characters so beautifully and empathically wrought. To experience the world as rendered by Margot Livesey is a singular, extraordinary delight."

—Claire Lombardo, author of *The Most Fun We Ever Had*

"A distinctive blend of literary fiction and psychological thriller. . . . Precise prose, cool observation, and tight pacing will keep readers turning the pages. This is a memorable twist on the coming-of-age tale."   —*Publishers Weekly*

"Compelling in its simplicity and complexity. Each page is rich with understanding of how lives fit together and fall apart."

—*Bookreporter*

"Written with psychological precision and empathy. . . . Explores the enduring and, in this case, elastic bonds of family love."

—*Bookpage*

THE BOY IN THE FIELD

ALSO BY MARGOT LIVESEY

THE BOY IN THE FIELD

A NOVEL

MARGOT LIVESEY

HARPER ● PERENNIAL

NEW YORK ● LONDON ● TORONTO ● SYDNEY ● NEW DELHI ● AUCKLAND

HARPER PERENNIAL

A hardcover edition of this book was published in 2020 by HarperCollins Publishers.

FIRST HARPER PERENNIAL EDITION PUBLISHED IN 2021.

The Library of Congress has catalogued the hardcover edition as follows:
Names: Livesey, Margot, author.
Title: The boy in the field: a novel / Margot Livesey.
Description: First edition. | New York: HarperCollins Publishers, [2020]
Identifiers: LCCN 2019045210 (print) | LCCN 2019045211 (ebook) | ISBN 9780062946393 (hardback) | ISBN 9780062946416 (ebook)
Subjects: LCSH: Domestic fiction.
Classification: LCC PR9199.3.L563 B69 2020 (print) | LCC PR9199.3.L563 (ebook) | DDC 813/.54—dc23
LC record available at https://lccn.loc.gov/2019045210
LC ebook record available at https://lccn.loc.gov/2019045211

ISBN 978-0-06-294640-9 (pbk.)

21 22 23 24 25   LSC   10 9 8 7 6 5 4 3 2 1

For Kathleen Hill

THE BOY IN THE FIELD

One

THE FIELD

HERE IS WHAT happened one Monday in the month of September, in the last year of the last century. Matthew, Zoe, and Duncan Lang were on their way home from school. Usually they took the bus from the larger town, where they attended secondary school, to the smaller town, where they lived, but that morning their father had said he had an errand to run and would collect them. So they waited beside the school gates, and watched the bus depart. After fifteen minutes, with no sign of the familiar car, they began to walk along the road that led to their town. They each wore a version of the school uniform: a white shirt, black trousers, and a black pullover. Expecting their father to appear at any moment, they walked fast, making it a game to see how far they could get before he pulled up beside them. They left the last houses behind. Hawthorn hedges and an occasional ash tree hid the fields that bordered the road. Through one gate they saw a herd of cows; through another, rows of barley. The afternoon was warm and still; only a few leaves fringed with brown hinted at autumn. Gnats hung in listless clouds above the tarmac. Zoe was the one who spotted something through the hedge. She had a gift for finding things: birds' nests, their mother's calculator, a missing book, a secret.

"What's that?" she demanded, stooping to peer through the tangled branches. The flash of red could have been poppies bordering the field, but the poppies had already lost their petals. Before her brothers could answer, she turned and ran back to the gate they had just passed.

Matthew and Duncan watched her go. Zoe brought her knees high and pumped her arms. Last sports day she had won the quarter mile by almost three seconds. As she reached the gate, Duncan, without a word, took off after her. A car sped by, the smooth engine noise undercut by a harsh rattle. Matthew looked at the sky, mostly blue with a fortress of cumulus clouds in the east, and gave up on being the responsible one who waited for their father. The two bags, his and Zoe's, banged against the metal bars of the gate as he climbed over and jumped down onto the rutted ground. The field had recently been harvested, and circular bales of straw lay randomly across the dull gold stubble. In the middle of the field stood a magnificent oak tree in full leaf. He caught up with first Duncan, then Zoe.

From a distance it was still possible to believe that the boy was asleep, lying on the grassy border between hedge and stubble. "Christ," whispered Zoe.

The closer they got to him, the slower they walked. None of them spoke. Glinting bluebottles and smaller flies circled the boy. His hair was dark, his skin very pale. He wore a deep blue shirt, a color Duncan would later call cobalt, black shorts, and what appeared to be long red socks. At the local private school, the younger boys wore bright red knee socks, and for the briefest instant, Zoe thought Oh, he's in uniform. A few steps closer, and she grasped the nature of the red. His eyelids were pale with a delicate tracery of veins. Everything that happened, they all three later agreed, was only possible because of those closed lids.

His chest rose, fractionally, and fell, fractionally. With no one to tell them what to feel, they did not cry out, or exclaim.

Zoe tiptoed forward, knelt down at a cautious distance, and leaned over to touch his bare arm where it emerged below his shirtsleeve. His skin was reassuringly warm. He was a little older than her. Eighteen. Perhaps nineteen. "We need to get help," she said.

But she was not going anywhere. She was gently stroking his bare arm.

Except for his clothes and his scarlet legs, Matthew thought, the boy could have been an illustration in a Victorian novel: *The Weary Harvester. Rest after Toil. The Dreaming Poet.* He told Duncan to go back to the road and stop a car. "Tell the driver someone's hurt," he said. "He needs an ambulance."

Duncan had been staring at the boy, committing him detail by detail, color by color, to memory. Now, reluctantly, he acknowledged the inevitability of being the youngest. He ran back along the edge of the field, scrambled over the gate again, and stood by the side of the road. In a well-organized world this would have been the moment for their father to arrive, driving, as usual, a little too fast.

The first car, black, sleek, ignored his frantic waving. So

did the second. The third car, baby blue, the antenna bent at an awkward angle, slowed. Duncan stepped into the road, ready to explain. The man behind the wheel—he too was wearing a white shirt—was staring at him through the dull windscreen. And then, just as the car seemed about to stop, it accelerated, swerved around him—he glimpsed the number plate and a dent in the rear bumper—and disappeared. It would have stopped for Zoe, he thought. Or even for Matthew. He shouldn't have let them send him to do this. But he had, and the beautiful boy was depending on him. At the sound of another car approaching, he planted himself in the middle of the road.

For a few scary seconds the car hurtled toward him. When the driver braked, he bent down at the window. "We found a boy in the field." He pointed behind him. "He's hurt."

"Hurt how?" The woman pushed up her sunglasses as if the emergency demanded naked sight. Her eyes were a color Duncan could only call colorless.

"I don't know. My brother says he needs an ambulance."

"Don't move him. I'll phone 999. Leave the gate of the field open so they'll know which one."

She did a U-turn in the gateway, and headed in the direction of the town.

Back in the field his sister was still stroking the boy's arm, his brother kneeling on the other side of him, fanning away the flies with a blue school notebook. They did not speak as he approached; he sensed they had not spoken during his absence.

"A woman's gone for help," he said, and knelt beside Zoe. His shirt had pulled loose as he ran, and the hem grazed the grass. "What's the matter with him? Did he fall?"

"Maybe," Zoe said. While Duncan was summoning help, she had noticed that the boy's shorts were torn in several places: two holes in one leg, one near the waist, one in the other leg. Last autumn her mother had lectured her and her friend Moira about how, at fifteen, they had to be careful. "Don't walk around alone at night," she had said. "Don't accept lifts from strangers. If a grown-up starts behaving oddly, find an excuse to leave."

"Oddly how?" Zoe had asked.

"Making remarks about your appearance, touching you." Her mother waved her hand. "Making you feel weird."

Alone, she and Moira had giggled away the warning, but now her mother's words came back; she tried not to think about the torn fabric—what made the holes, what lay beneath. From beyond the hedge came the sounds of a car approaching, disappearing, then another. "Do we know him?" she asked.

"I don't," Matthew said. As he moved the notebook, the flies retreated with almost military precision and, with the same precision, returned. Everything was warm and frightening. The boy was alive, which meant he might die. He was not sure Zoe and Duncan understood that.

"Maybe he looks different?" Zoe persisted. "Perhaps we've seen him at the shops, or on the bus?"

Matthew was still shaking his head—that the boy's life might have touched theirs only made the idea of his death more frightening—when Duncan spoke. If Zoe was the one who found things, their little brother was the one who noticed them: the different yellows of two egg yolks, the way a person's lips twitched when they met him, the first snowdrops pushing up through the frosty grass, the curve of a dog's eyebrows. Matthew had asked Zoe once if she thought Duncan was better at noticing things because he was adopted. No, she had said, because he's Duncan.

Now Duncan said, "I've seen him before, but I'm not sure where."

Looking at the boy, he too thought of a picture, a painting his art teacher had shown him of a wide-eyed, cream-colored bull climbing into the sky with a girl on his back. Zeus had courted Europa by breathing out a saffron crocus from his dark nostrils. Who could resist a flower born of such sweetness? Not Europa. She had clambered onto his back, thinking to ride him around the meadow, garland him with flowers, only to find the bull carrying her skyward toward unknown terror, or unknown bliss. Had something like that happened to the boy?

"If his eyes were open," Zoe said, "I bet you'd remember."

If his eyes were open, Matthew thought, we would not be kneeling here. He would be in pain, and we couldn't bear it. How long had they been here? Ten minutes? Twenty? He glanced over his shoulder at the nearest bale. Last autumn he and his friend Benjamin had carried a ladder out to the field behind Benjamin's house, climbed up onto a stack of bales, and shared a beer. It had been oddly satisfying, sitting on the prickly straw, watching the lights of the town appear. Now, still fanning the boy, he edged closer. His left knee landed on something soft: a spiraling strip, maybe eight inches long, of brownish apple peel. He tossed it in the direction of the oak tree.

"You're going to be all right," Zoe said.

The boy gave a small sigh. His lips moved. The sigh became a word.

Each of them caught it.

No more words followed.

Two swallows swooped past, skimming the air above their heads. Briefly Duncan imagined the scene as if he were riding not on a bull but on the back of one of the birds, looking down at the boy lying in the grass, his blue shirt and black shorts and red legs ending in black trainers, slightly dusty, pointing at the sky. And the three of them in their white shirts, kneeling beside him, keeping vigil. When he descended again, it was with a longing to memorize every detail of the boy. He had seldom had license to examine another person so closely. Years later he would remember him more vividly than men and women he had loved, friends he had adored.

His hair was shoulder length, wavy, the brown of soil after rain; his forehead was high; his nose straight with an almost invisible bump at the bridge; his nostrils, against his pale skin, were faintly pink; his lips were parted, the upper a little fuller; his ears, shell-like, lay close to his head; the left had a tiny dark hole in the lobe. A thin silver chain lay across the hollow between his collarbones. He wore a watch, the black leather strap faded and cracked. His hands were open, palms up, his fingers gently curved.

Duncan was still itemizing the boy when there was a commotion in the road: the sounds of a vehicle stopping, doors opening, voices, and then three men hurrying down the edge of the field, one carrying a stretcher.

NO ONE HAD MENTIONED THE children, and no provision had been made for them. One of the paramedics called "All right there?" over his shoulder as they hurried toward the gate with their burden. "Fine," Matthew called back. By the time the three of them reached the gate, the ambulance was gone.

They half walked, half ran, the rest of the way home. Something enormous had happened. They hurried past the sign for their town, the primary school they had each attended, the church, the pub, and the corner shop, past the houses of their neighbors, past the blowsy yellow and white roses in their front garden and through their blue front door. As it closed behind them, their father, Hal, appeared from the kitchen, an apron around his waist, a dish towel dangling from one hand. He was a blacksmith or, as he sometimes joked, an artisanal metalworker, and usually got home earlier than their mother to make supper.

"Where on earth did you get to?" he said. "I waited at the school. Then the caretaker told me you were walking home. I didn't see you on the road. Did you get a lift?"

His blue eyes were more amused than annoyed, but as Zoe and Matthew took turns recounting what had happened, they darkened. "Wait a minute," he interrupted. "This boy, he'd been taken ill? He'd had an accident?"

Zoe described the holes in the boy's shorts, the blood on his legs.

"I think someone stabbed him," Matthew offered.

"Stabbed him?" Duncan said. It hadn't occurred to him to wonder how the boy came to be lying there, but Matthew must be right. Someone had made the blood spill down his legs.

"Did anyone phone the police?" Their father was looking at each of them in turn as if, collectively, they might be to blame.

Duncan said he hadn't mentioned the police to the woman in the car. "Was I meant to?"

Still holding the dish towel, their father said he thought he'd give the station in Oxford a call, and stepped over to the phone.

AT SUPPER, THE FIVE OF them sitting around their round table, their mother, Betsy, made them tell the story again. "Thank goodness you found him," she said. "Who knows what might have happened."

"He'd have died," said Zoe severely. "We have five or six quarts of blood in our bodies. If we lose five or six pints, we die." She glared at her plate, the meek fish pie and green beans. Then, turning to her brothers, she said, "Do you think the person who attacked him was still there? Do you think he saw us?"

Separately and together, each of them considered: Had someone been lurking behind one of the bales? Peering down through the leaves of the oak tree?

"Someone could have hidden behind a bale," Duncan said, "but I don't think they did." The field had felt the way their house did after Arthur, the dachshund, died: empty.

"And didn't you say he'd been there for a while?" said their mother. She was a solicitor, who dealt mostly with family law, and an ardent advocate for children's rights.

It was true, Matthew thought, the boy looked as if he'd been lying there for hours, but none of them had actually said so. Their mother, like the witnesses she so often complained about, was making assumptions. "But why would someone want to hurt him?" he demanded.

Their parents exchanged glances.

"Maybe he got in an argument," their mother suggested. "Maybe he stole something?" Her eyebrows rose toward her reddish-brown hair; people often thought she dyed it.

Duncan put down his fork. No one with such shell-like ears could be a thief.

"Or maybe"—their father too was imagining the scene—"it was about sex." He was the parent they could count on not to worry that they were too young to hear certain things. The x of "sex" tinkled against the salt and pepper shakers.

At the school Christmas party last year Matthew had kissed Rachel in the cloakroom for forty-five minutes. He had had other girlfriends—three of them—but they had in no way prepared him for the astonishing discovery that bodies, his own, another person's, could be the source of such endless pleasure.

"What your father means," their mother said, "is that there are people who are wired differently, who get a thrill out of doing bad things, but they're very few, and far between." She was still wearing the suit she often wore in court. Duncan claimed it was the color of old potatoes.

"We're not children." Zoe speared a green bean. "We know about perverts. Some person, some man, dragged the boy into a field, or got him to follow him, and then he stabbed him. That person could be living in our street. He could be walking past our house right now."

On the word "now," the doorbell rang. Each of them startled. Their father half rose, looked around the table, counting—one, two, three, four—and went to answer. Few people passing Hal in the street would have guessed his strength; he was five foot eleven, square-shouldered and tightly muscled, but Matthew had seen him lift a car out of a ditch, bend an iron bar into shape.

"Don't—" their mother started to say, and stopped. They were not going to become a family who didn't answer their door.

On the doorstep stood a man whose pale shirt, dark jacket, and dark trousers were as much a uniform as that worn by the policewoman standing behind him. He introduced himself as Detective Hugh Price and apologized for the timing of his visit.

"I understand, Mr. Lang, that your children found a young man, wounded, in a field."

Hal showed them into the room they jokingly called the parlor. He and Betsy had furnished it as a dining room and then ended up, even when they had guests, eating in the kitchen. A stack of boxes stood in one corner, and the table was piled with bills. Next to the computer, taking up almost as much space, was a model of the set Zoe had made last spring when she was the stage manager for *Antony and Cleopatra*. Against one wall stood the upright piano on which only Duncan still took lessons; from the top Matthew's fencing mask blindly observed the room. Hal moved the bills and pulled out two chairs. Back in the kitchen, he dispatched Matthew to answer the detective's questions.

During the long summers when he was becoming a teenager, Matthew had read scores of detective novels. Along with many TV programs, they had given him an image of this tribe of men who drank too much, shaved too little, were oddly erudite, seldom happily married, and in general behaved more like the villains they were trying to catch than the citizens they were trying to protect. Often they had some arcane hobby: growing roses, listening to opera. At first sight Hugh Price contradicted most of these notions. He wore a wedding ring, and even at eight in the evening his fair skin was smoothly shaved. His triangular face—like a Siamese cat's, Duncan said later—balanced on a long, elegant neck. He offered Matthew his hand, and introduced himself and PC Hannah Jones. Beneath her hat, her hair was wavy, and her eyebrows swooped like dark wings. She was, Matthew judged, only a few years older than him.

As he gave his full name and age, he felt his palms grow slippery. I'm not guilty, he thought indignantly, but his body had its own ideas. "How is he?" he said.

The detective said the boy had recovered consciousness. "The doctors expect him to make a full recovery. Can you tell me, in your own words, what happened this afternoon?"

Briefly Matthew pictured other people's words hanging in the air: laundry on a washing line. He could borrow one person's pajamas, another's T-shirt. He explained about their father not showing up at the school, how they had started to walk home.

The detective paused in his rearranging of the miniature columns in Zoe's set. "You don't usually walk?"

"No. It's nearly five miles. We take the bus. Sometimes we cycle."

"Did you see anything lying by the side of the road? Pass any cars? Or cyclists? Other people walking?"

A number of cars had passed, one cyclist that he recalled, a man in sleek shorts, pedaling hard, but no other pedestrians. They had been discussing what to give their mother for her birthday. Zoe wanted to get her a necklace; Duncan had seen a print he liked in an antique shop. The afternoon had been entirely ordinary until Zoe spotted something through the hedge, and he and Duncan followed her into the field.

"Was the gate open? Were there any marks on it? Anything unusual?"

Matthew yearned to be helpful, but all he remembered was the surprising newness of the gate. He shook his head, no.

"And did you recognize the boy?"

"Duncan, my brother, thought he'd seen him before but he couldn't remember where. Do you know who he is?"

"His name is Karel Lustig. He works nights at the Cottage Hospital." The detective let the name occupy the room before he asked his next question. "When you saw him, did anything strike you?"

"He looked very peaceful. We thought he was asleep."

They had, but only for a few seconds. The boy had lain so still. The detective remarked his hesitation and he admitted that what the boy really reminded him of was a statue at Dorchester Abbey: John de Stonor, lying on his tomb, his marble clothing neatly arranged for eternity. Sitting next to the detective, the constable made a note. Had Matthew finally said something of interest, or had she just remembered that she needed to buy eggs?

"Did you touch him?"

Matthew shook his head again; he had wanted to. "Zoe did."

"And did he speak?"

"Once. He said 'Coward.'"

Through the open window a sudden breeze caught the overhead light; their three shadows swayed back and forth across the piano. Matthew imagined their house, all the houses in the street, in the town, empty of people, like the ruined mansion they had come across in Wales last summer, the rooms decorated with flowery wallpaper, ivy creeping through the windows.

When their shadows quieted, the detective said, "So, were there any signs, besides his injuries, that another person had been there? That there'd been a fight?"

He recalled the boy's hands lying on the grass, empty. He himself often went out with only the contents of his pockets, but when he was going to school, or to his job at the Co-op, he always had a backpack. "He didn't have anything with him," he said. "Maybe that was a sign of another person?"

The detective was nodding. According to a nurse at the Cottage Hospital, Karel had been carrying a backpack when he left work and discovered that his bicycle had a flat tire. "Whoever picked him up was probably the same person who attacked him and took his bag. We'll know more when he's conscious."

Matthew heard the "probably." "Are you saying someone found him before us, stole his bag, and left him there?" In books and films, the villain nearly always turned out to be not the obvious person.

"No, but it's important not to take anything for granted. Do you fence?" The detective nodded at the mask on top of the piano.

"I'm taking lessons."

"Épée or foil?"

"Foil, so far."

"If you remember anything else, no matter how small, please get in touch. Don't worry about bothering me, or seeming stupid." He held out a business card, the first Matthew had ever been offered. Then, tilting his triangular face, the detective said, "You did a good thing today. You saved a boy's life."

WHILE MATTHEW TALKED TO THE detective, his father, back at the kitchen table, helped himself to more fish pie—it had turned out well—and described his latest commission, a wrought-iron garden gate. He had persuaded the customer to let him use William Morris's willow pattern.

"Nice," said Duncan. "Lots of little leaves."

Shut up, shut up, Zoe thought. Why was the detective taking so long? What could Matthew possibly have to say? Her impatience shredded the air. She pulled the elastic band off her ponytail, shook out her hair. When Duncan stood to clear the plates, she stayed in her chair. She could do nothing but wait.

At last Matthew returned. As she stepped into the parlor, she felt her shoulders relax, her heartbeat slow. This man would explain what had happened; he would make sense of the boy's scarlet legs. He introduced himself and asked her full name and age. While the policewoman wrote down her answers, he absentmindedly plucked Cleopatra's barge from the blue ribbon of the Nile that ran across the back of the set, behind the Forum.

"Could you tell me about this afternoon?" he said.

She gave her account, trying to be as precise as possible, and asked if the boy was going to be all right. The detective said he would be fine in a few weeks. Without prompting, he told her the boy's name—pleasingly distinct—and occupation.

"But why would anyone hurt him?" she said. "Are there really people who drive around at seven a.m., waiting to stab hospital orderlies?"

He cradled Cleopatra's barge; in his long fingers, it looked like a large canoe. "Perhaps they had an argument? Your brother said you touched him."

Was he accusing her? She couldn't tell. "I wanted him to know he wasn't alone. I didn't hurt him."

"I'm sure he appreciated that. Did he say anything while you were with him?"

"He said 'Cowrie.' Like the little shells the Vikings used as money." On her desk she had an eggcup half full of the ones she'd collected on the beach in Wales.

" 'Cowrie,' you're sure?"

Zoe said she was—maybe he was dreaming? Both the detective and the police constable wrote in their notebooks. "Please phone," he said, "if you remember anything else."

She slipped his card into her pocket. "Do you mind putting my barge back?"

THAT NIGHT DUNCAN TURNED OFF the lights in his room and stood at the window, staring down into the shadowy garden. Their house was in the middle of a terrace, the garden separated from those of their neighbors by brick walls. Beyond the lawn and the picnic table was a pergola covered with roses and honeysuckle, and beyond that a bed of rhododendrons, azaleas, smoke bushes, and two laburnum trees. The breeze that had sprung up earlier had grown stronger, and the trees and shrubs were swaying. The boy's one word—"Cowslip"—had made him think of the little mermaid and her sisters, tending their gardens beneath the turquoise sea. When he was younger, eight or nine, he had read the story over and over, picturing the garden filled with cornflowers and cowslips, willing the prince to recognize the little mermaid. Now, as he stood watching, a person stepped forward beneath the laburnum trees.

My first mother, he thought. She's come for me.

For years he had seldom spoken of his birth mother, rarely thought of her, but not for a second did he doubt his vision. She was summoning him, warning him. Even as he pressed his face to the glass, the dark form faded, thinned, became another shadow among shadows.

Everyone else was in bed. Walking as quietly as possible, he went downstairs and made his way from room to room. He had always liked windows—the eyes of a house, giving and receiving light—but as he checked each lock, they seemed stupidly fragile. One stone, and anyone could climb in. Once again he missed Arthur, who had announced each visitor with a single low bark.

Back in his room, he wedged a chair under the doorknob like people did in films. Still he did not turn on the light, which would betray his presence, or the radio. Lying in bed, he felt guilt creeping up his arms. He was leaving his parents and siblings undefended. Worse than that. He was hoping that any intruder would be waylaid by more tempting choices. When the guilt reached his shoulders, he got out of bed and moved the chair back to his desk.

Two

MATTHEW

HIS FIRST WAKING thought was that yesterday he had encountered something extraordinary: a crime like the ones he read about in books, with a victim and a villain. Gazing at his bedroom window, the curtains fringed with light, he was filled with elation. But as he got up, washed, and dressed in the predictable school uniform, the feeling ebbed. Today, he could already tell, was going to be what he and Benjamin called the SOS: same old shit. Downstairs he found Duncan at the table, yawning over his cornflakes, and their mother at the counter, making her lunch.

Zoe was hovering beside the toaster. "Please can we have the day off?" she begged. "You could say we were in an accident."

He was about to object—he had spent hours preparing for the debate in history, and he needed to see Rachel—but their mother was already saying she didn't think half an hour in a field justified their absence. "Don't forget your running shoes," she added.

He waited to see how Zoe would respond. Often his sister treated argument as a sport, persisting long after the outcome was settled. Now he watched her watch their mother, as she deftly wrapped her sandwich, and decide not to press her case.

On the bus they each usually sat with friends. Today he slid into the seat beside Zoe; Duncan took the seat in front. Opening his history book, he tried to focus on Archduke Ferdinand and the numerous and confusing causes of World War I. Duncan and Zoe got out their own books. Last night, before he left, the detective had asked them not to talk about the boy in the field. "You walked home from school and did your homework," he had said. "End of story." As the bus neared the school, Zoe reminded them of their promise.

"Who would I talk to?" Duncan said.

It was not, Matthew knew, a rhetorical question. His brother was genuinely curious: Who, among his friends, did Zoe consider a suitable confidant?

"Just don't," she said. Although she was the one who would find it hard not to chatter to Moira and Frances and Gita.

Inside the school they had no choice but to separate. As he got out his French textbook, the girl at the next desk asked if he'd heard. A boy had been attacked in a field and nearly died. "Didn't you walk home yesterday?" she said.

He was simultaneously nodding and shaking his head when Mademoiselle Fournier came to the rescue. "Bonjour, mes élèves. Comment ça va?"

As he went from class to class, he heard different versions of the story: a boy had been assaulted, murdered, robbed at gunpoint, sometimes two boys. By the time he saw Rachel at lunchtime, he was able to feign ordinary curiosity. She repeated the gun story, and he said he had heard that too. Only Benjamin didn't mention the boy; he had had an idea for their next event. For the last year the two of them had been staging odd happenings: an anarchic egg-and-spoon race at sports day; a stall outside the gym selling artisanal paper clips; an imaginary country inserted on the map in the geography classroom. Six weeks had passed before anyone noticed Wallenia, complete with mountains, lakes, and a capital city, overlapping Bulgaria and Romania.

Now Benjamin suggested a millennium display. "We could have all kinds of machines failing," he said. "Pencil sharpeners, lawn mowers, eggbeaters, alarm clocks."

"Toasters," Matthew volunteered, "hair dryers, staplers."

Was a stall at school the best idea? Or maybe in town, outside the Co-op? It was a relief, as they traded ideas, not to think about the boy for ten minutes.

That afternoon Duncan had a piano lesson, and Zoe was at cross-country; he sat alone near the front of the bus. The temperature had fallen, and the sky tumbled with the gray clouds that his father called cumulonimbus capillatus. Soon the swallows would gather on the telegraph wires, getting ready for their long flight south. When he'd told Zoe about Wallenia, she had said, "But what's the point, if no one notices?" That, he had tried to explain, was exactly the point.

He got off at the stop beside the Co-op. Through the plate glass window, he could see Eileen and Bob on the tills, ringing up customers. He waved, and Bob waved back. At the first corner he turned not toward home but in the direction of his father's forge, a few streets away. The double doors facing onto the forecourt were closed, which meant no more customers were expected that day. He let himself in by the side door. The forge had been in the family for over a hundred years, and no one, not even his father, knew the exact contents of the building. There were horseshoes from when Queen Victoria was on the throne, account books kept in elegant copperplate, tools that should have been in a museum, lists of jobs and debts, faded calendars, single gloves, coils of wire, cigar boxes full of nails, old bellows, hammers, and vises of many sizes. This afternoon the fire was almost out, his father's apprentice had gone home, and his father was standing at the workbench, sorting nails into a row of boxes. Matthew watched his hands moving back and forth. When he was younger, he had found his parents' ability to concentrate bewildering. What did it mean that he disappeared so entirely from their brains? Now he envied them.

"Hi, Dad."

"Matthew. I didn't hear you come in. You'd make a good burglar."

"Have they caught the man?"

"The man?" His father reached for a handful of nails. "Oh, you mean whoever attacked that boy. How would I know? I've been here all day, working on my willow gate." He dropped three nails into three different compartments—each landed with a different clink—and glanced over at Matthew. "Don't worry," he said. "He won't attack anyone else."

All day thoughts about the boy and his assailant had been

sliding in and out of Matthew's brain, but that the man might seek another victim had not been among them. Now his father saying he wouldn't at once raised the specter that he would. He imagined the man lying in wait in some doorway, or behind a tree. His father was still talking. Zoe was the one he worried about. She was impulsive, overly confident. And she could easily pass for older. "You've got to keep an eye on her," he urged, "especially when she doesn't want you to."

Two summers ago, when they were camping in Normandy, Zoe had failed to return from buying baguettes. They had searched the campsite, the town. Just as their mother was about to call the police, she had reappeared. The guide from the local museum, whom they'd befriended the day before, had been at the boulangerie; he had taken her to see a World War II bunker. "It had these tiny windows for guns," she said. "And a hole in the ceiling for a periscope."

"Promise you won't go off with a stranger again," their mother had said. "Anything could have happened."

Zoe had promised but, watching her face, Matthew could tell she didn't understand the force of "anything." Only in the last few months, as he and Rachel spent more and more time beneath her duvet, had he sensed that his sister too, with the help of first Luke, then Ant, was learning this new language.

"Dad, she never listens to me. Besides, you said he wouldn't attack anyone else."

"Well, do your best," said his father. "I'll be home soon. Betsy's at her class until eight."

His mother's class in ancient Greek was a new addition to the family timetable. In August she had announced that she'd always wanted to read *The Odyssey* in the original. Now twice a week she came home late, and at weekends she did homework at the kitchen table, frowning over the unfamiliar alphabet.

The lattice of streets between the forge and their house was so familiar that often Matthew walked the entire distance noticing nothing. Today he silently interrogated the houses and privet hedges, the cars and cats and rowan trees. Do you know Karel? Do you know who hurt him? And then, as he passed the plaque marking the site of the old glove makers' factory, he was thinking not about Karel but about Claire. She had joined his class halfway through primary six, and their teacher had asked him to show her round. She was older than him, almost eleven, and wanted to go to Iceland where there were volcanoes and wild ponies.

One day she had invited him home for tea. They had played Monopoly with her little sisters, who were too young to follow the rules but liked shaking the dice. Claire was negotiating for Pall Mall when a car pulled up in the street. The next thing he knew, she was folding the Monopoly board into the box, telling her sisters to be quiet and Matthew to do his homework. "What's all the fuss?" he had said. Then her father came into the room.

All he could think was: I have to get out of here.

"But did he do something?" his mother asked when he tried to explain.

"He said good evening and looked at me like I was a worm."

Next day, when Claire raised her hand in class, he had glimpsed a bracelet of bruises. "If I were you," he had said at break, "I'd run away."

"Where to?" she said bitterly. "Iceland? Besides I can't leave my sisters behind."

His mother said she would speak to the head teacher, but unless the father did something drastic, they couldn't intervene. "You mean," Matthew said, "he has to hurt Claire before we can stop him hurting her?" He had begun walking her home every afternoon, hoping to be invited in. If only her father would hit him, they could go to the police. But she always said goodbye at the end of the street. Then one Monday her desk was empty. The teacher announced that Claire's family had moved to Bristol.

He was almost at the house. There was the pillar box, and the cherry tree his mother watered in summer. Surely by now, he thought, Claire had taken his advice and fled. Inside the empty hall, he turned on the light, took out the detective's card, and went over to the phone. A woman answered on the second ring, and then Hugh Price was saying, "Matthew. Did you remember something?"

"No," he said sheepishly. Of course the detective would think he'd called with information. "I was wondering if you'd caught whoever did it?"

"Not yet. But we have a good description."

"So he's out there, walking around?" He tried, and failed, to conceal his indignation.

There was a ticking sound, as if the workings of the detective's brain were suddenly audible. When he spoke again, he sounded tired. "He may have bolted, or gone to ground, but yes, chances are, he's just going about his business."

After he replaced the receiver, Matthew studied the phone with its ten numbers, which could be combined into thousands, millions, of permutations. If the man had a phone, then one of those permutations would ring in his living room, or hall. He pictured himself dialing, and dialing, and dialing.

Three

DUNCAN

DURING ENGLISH, MS. Humphreys gave them fifteen minutes to answer the questions she'd written on the board about *The Merchant of Venice*. Then she collected their notebooks and walked around at the front of the room, calling on different pupils. When she looked in his direction, he closed his eyes; she asked the girl in front. At the end of the lesson she gave him a little nod and came to sit at the next desk. In a low voice, quite different from the one she'd been using to address the class, she asked if he had read the play.

He had.

"Did you side with Shylock, or Antonio?"

"Both. Shylock was cruel—the idea of cutting a pound of flesh is horrible—but Antonio treated him as if he had no feelings. And then Jessica steals from him and runs away."

"And what about the caskets?"

"They were just a way for Portia's father to control her, and make the suitors seem dumb. It had to be the lead casket."

"But you only answered two of the questions." Ms. Humphreys held up his open notebook.

Someone had drawn a seagull on a corner of the desk. Nearby was a rudimentary cat. Duncan saw how each could be made better. Following his gaze, Ms. Humphreys said, "Could you have drawn the answers?"

"If I had enough time, if people didn't keep interrupting. If . . ." How to explain that sometimes a drawing came right the first time. Sometimes it took a dozen attempts, and even then failed.

"Do you know what a self-fulfilling prophecy is? If you keep doing badly on tests, you start expecting to do badly, and then you do even worse. You just need more time."

"So I'm not"—he retrieved an insult from last year—"a moron?"

He saw Ms. Humphreys register the word, and the context in which he must have heard it. "No," she said firmly. "You have a good brain, but you're going to have to learn to stand up for yourself, to explain that some things take you longer. I know you're passionate about painting, but you need words too."

ON THE BUS HOME HE saw Zoe sitting halfway back and went to join her. He was longing to tell her about Ms. Humphreys and his good brain, but she was folding and unfolding her shirt cuffs, a sure sign of fretfulness. "Do you remember," she said as the bus pulled away from the school, "when the Sawyers' dog attacked you?"

How could he forget one of the worst events of his life that had led to one of the best? He and Zoe were playing in the Sawyers' garden—their mother was having tea with Mrs. Sawyer—when the back door opened and a huge dog leaped across the lawn and, in a single motion, seized Duncan's leg. The pain was blinding, deafening. From far away he heard Zoe yelling. Later she showed him the red tooth mark on her hand where the dog had briefly released him to snap at her. Then Mrs. Sawyer was standing over them, shouting, "Let go, Leo. Let go."

The day his stitches came out, his father had arrived home with a dachshund. "He'll help you get over being afraid of dogs," he had said, and Arthur, small, wise, the color of a newly hulled chestnut, with dark ears and a beautiful smile, had turned out to be the perfect ambassador for dogkind. He had carefully distributed his favors among the five of them, with a marked preference for Duncan.

"So why didn't you scream?" Zoe said now as the bus swayed around a corner.

His trousers hid the crescent scar, but he could picture the seventeen tooth marks; the boy had had two red stockings, he had had one. "He was eating my leg," he said. "All I could do was try to disappear."

"Did you hear anything? See anyone?"

"You mean, besides you screaming and Leo growling? No, there was a kind of haze."

"Remember that TV program about people who nearly died and saw a bright light at the end of a tunnel, someone waiting to welcome them? Do you think Karel saw someone?"

Duncan didn't remember the program, but he did remember the boy's pale eyelids. "No."

"Perhaps"—Zoe smoothed her cuffs—"he was waiting for the right person to wake him."

From the way she spoke, both halting and eager, he knew she wanted to be that person. He himself had felt no desire to wake Karel. Watching the vein pulsing in his temple, his chest rising and falling, he had sensed that the boy had made his way to a place of safety; to wake him would be to hurl him back into hardship. Before he could say any of this, Moira was standing over them. Would Zoe like to go to the cinema?

The autumn Leo had tried to eat his leg was also the autumn his father's mother had come to live with them. Every afternoon, when he got home from nursery, he would go to the sitting room to show Granny the paintings he had made that day, and she would reward him with one of her special cough sweets, a purple oval dusted in sugar. "Your pictures emanate," she told him. He asked what that meant, and she said, "They reach out to people. They glow." But one afternoon her armchair was empty. He had looked in the parlor, the kitchen, before he knocked on her bedroom door. As he opened it very quietly—he was doing something forbidden—he heard a strange noise. Still holding onto the doorknob, he had stood there, searching the wardrobe, the windows, the heavy curtains, the chest of drawers, until, at last, he understood that it was Granny, lying in bed, who was making the hoarse rattling sounds that filled the room.

His mother had discovered him, kneeling beside her. Later, alone in his room, he had drawn her pointed nose and sunken cheeks, her closed eyes and open mouth. Normally he didn't care who saw his drawings—they were his, and not his—but this one he hid.

Four

ZOE

SHE WAS STILL going to school, still studying, joking around with Moira, doing her chores, but it was as if her hair had stopped growing. A change, invisible to most other people, had overtaken her. A few days after they found the boy, she was searching for a book about Florence Nightingale when she came across a poem she had written the previous spring about her grandfather. She had carried her notebook to the churchyard and, sitting beneath a yew tree, summoned her memories: his mustache yellow with nicotine, his collection of fountain pens, the poems he recited when they went on walks, his interest in airplanes, his dislike of his given name, Horace. She reread her first line: *When we first met, I was the unsteady one*. According to family lore, Horry had taught her to walk, holding her hand as she tipsily crossed the lawn.

She had been working on the third stanza when a man, a stranger, came through the gate on the far side of the church-yard. What she saw first was his panama hat, then his white shirt and jeans. He was carrying a book. She had a vivid sense of the picture she made, a girl sitting beneath a yew tree, writing a possibly immortal sonnet. Perhaps the man was a scholar, searching the churchyard for some historical figure. Or a visitor looking for his own grandfather. The hat made him look vaguely foreign.

She was struggling with the lines about her grandfather returning to the battlefields of his youth, when she felt a kind of buzzing. The man was standing thirty feet away, between two gravestones, his eyes fixed not on her but on the yew tree, his arms motionless at his sides. She glanced at his face and then—he was willing it—glanced lower.

Everything happened very quickly. She saw his jeans and something that was not his jeans. The man retreated behind a gravestone. His shoulders hunched—fastening his fly, she guessed—and he walked swiftly, not quite running, toward the gate.

She tried to continue writing about her grandfather, barely twenty, trapped in a muddy foxhole, but after a few minutes she set aside her notebook and walked over to the gravestones. The man had left his book on top of the taller stone: A. E. Housman's *A Shropshire Lad*. "Loveliest of trees, the cherry now" was one of her grandfather's favorite poems.

"A flasher," Moira had said when she told her. "He must have been thrilled, finding a nubile girl in the churchyard."

"But what was the point? He showed me his willy and ran away."

"The point was to shock somebody."

Not somebody, Zoe had thought: me. The man had come to

the churchyard to read, or look for a grave, and then, at the sight of her, been unable to help himself, like Antony with Cleopatra, giving up an empire for a kiss. Now, looking at the poem, it ended midway through the tenth line, she thought maybe she could go back to it. Or write another poem, about the boy lying on the grass while the birds watched over him.

Five

MATTHEW

HE HAD WORRIED he might not recognize the gate, one among many, but a loop of yellow police tape hung helpfully from the top bar. He wheeled his bike into the field and leaned it against the hedge. The bales were still there, mysteriously larger. The oak tree looked the same, dark and burly. No swallows today—had they already left?—but two magpies strutting across the stubble, tails jerking. On the grass near the gate lay a gray stick, abandoned by some hiker.

He carried the stick over to where he remembered the boy lying and began to circle it. All day he had imagined finding something significant: a key, a pair of spectacles, a business card reading *John Smith, Assailant*. In the books he read, there were always clues. His father had told him the word "clue" came from the Anglo-Saxon for thread, and that was what he was looking for, a thread that would lead him from something small, something everyone else had overlooked, to another thing and another, each a step closer to finding the assailant. Scrutinizing the ground, he saw only grass, knobbly soil, straw, pebbles, rabbit droppings.

The month before, on a picnic, his mother had lost her wedding ring. One moment the five of them were talking and laughing. The next they were crawling around, searching. Nothing. Nothing. Then Zoe had exclaimed "Here it is," and they were all laughing again, the gap between disaster and happiness instantly closed. He picked a few blades of grass and slipped them into his shirt pocket. When he got home, he would write the date on an envelope and seal the grass inside. He pictured men in uniform on their hands and knees, with magnifying glasses and metal detectors. If there were anything to find, wouldn't they have found it? To his left he saw a flash of black and white: the magpies taking flight. The air shifted, and the first drops of rain fell.

Near the hedge he discovered an empty beer bottle, coated with mud, a crumpled page from a comic Zoe used to read, and the dull blue rectangle of a local bus ticket. The last he put in his pocket, beside the blades of grass. He was walking back to the gate, the soil already darkening with rain, when he remembered the stick. Turning to retrieve it, he caught a glint of silver. There, beside a tuft of grass, lay the boy's silver chain. It must have fallen, unnoticed, as the paramedics carried him to the gate. When he picked it up, he saw that the chain held a medallion the size of a ten-pence coin: a man fording a river with a small haloed figure on his shoulder.

AT HOME HE HEADED TO Zoe's room, eager to show the St. Christopher. She was at her desk, doing homework; Duncan was lying on her bed, drawing. "Hi," they both said without looking up. One of Matthew's earliest memories was of the day his parents had brought home a tiny being with silky hair and perfect hands. His new brother had gazed, waveringly, at some distant view. Then his brown eyes had found Matthew and settled on him with a look of deep attention. Now, watching Duncan's pencil move across the page, he could not remember the last time his brother had visited his room. Had he been curt? Preoccupied? As he zigzagged through the clutter on Zoe's floor, he vowed to make amends. He picked up the dictionary on the window seat, and sat down.

Duncan's pencil paused. "What does 'raped' mean?" he said.

Christ, thought Matthew. How to explain? He opened the dictionary, searching for the Rs, but Zoe was already offering her definition.

"One person," she said, "usually a man, forces another person, usually a woman, to do it, but it's not really doing it."

"You do it"—Duncan started to draw again—"but you don't?"

She walked over to the bed. "Give me your hand."

Matthew watched as she began to squeeze, at first gently, then more and more tightly until Duncan cried "Stop."

"Like that. Something that can be good becomes bad because only one person wants it. Do you think"—she twirled so that her hair flew around her shoulders—"the man would have stopped to give me a lift?"

Last spring, when she and Matthew missed the bus, she had been the one to hold out her arm and smile at the invisible motorists rushing by. Barely a dozen cars passed before a woman pulled over. As she accelerated back onto the road, she had asked if their parents knew what they were doing. "Yes," Zoe had said, so quickly that all Matthew could do was nod.

"Zoe," he said now, "you're mad. Whoever did this was seriously messed up. He would have driven right past you."

"Because I'm not pretty enough? Old enough?"

Looking at her bright top, her faded jeans, he recalled his father's admonition. She had changed so much in the last year, and in the few days since they knelt in the field, she had changed again. Perhaps something had traveled from Karel's arm into her outstretched hand. He knew of several boys at school who liked her. Would they stop liking the new Zoe? Or like her even more? He suspected the latter.

"Because," he said, getting to his feet, "no one would want to hurt you." Somehow the moment to show the St. Christopher had passed.

"WAS THERE ANYTHING ELSE YOU wanted to tell me?" the detective said. They were in his office in the police station on St. Aldate's, the St. Christopher lying on the desk between them. As he spoke, the telephone rang. Matthew waited for him to answer, and after half a dozen rings, realized he wasn't going to. No one had ever not answered a phone for him. Hugh Price was more like a TV detective than he had at first seemed. On the wall above his desk hung a black-and-white photograph of a row of cottages next to a snowy field. The ringing stopped.

"How is Karel?" Matthew said.

"He's home from the hospital. He's very grateful to the three of you."

"Did he describe the person who attacked him?"

"Caucasian man, brown hair, clean shaven, blue eyes, reddish cheeks, thirtyish, medium build, wearing a suit. West Country accent. Walk down any street in Oxford, at any time of day, and you'll see ten men who fit that description. If he has no prior convictions, which is often the case with a crime of passion, we're going to have to get lucky. Did you find anything else in the field?"

Don't *you* have any clues, Matthew wanted to say. "An empty beer bottle. And a bus ticket."

The latter was still in his pocket, and he handed it over. Hugh Price thanked him, and asked if they might take his fingerprints. In another room a woman rolled his thumbs and fingers one by one on a pad of ink and pressed them to a piece of paper, divided into ten rectangles.

"If you were planning a life of crime," the detective said, "I'm afraid this will make it harder."

Walking back to the bus station, Matthew counted nine men who fitted the description; on the bus were two more brown-haired, thirtyish, white men. None wore a suit. He sat down next to a girl in school uniform, a book open on her lap. As she read, she gently whisked the end of her braid back and forth across the page: stroking the words? keeping herself company? There were several girls at school who behaved like this, treating their hair as if it were a silent, always available pet. Rachel, happily, was not among them.

Six

DUNCAN

HE WAS AT the piano, playing "Greensleeves," when the door-bell rang. Zoe and Matthew were out with friends, his mother was walking with her hiking group. He paused, listening for his father's footsteps, and hearing them, started to play again. A minute later came a rap on the door. "Duncan, can you come and say hello?"

In the kitchen a man with beautiful golden eyebrows and fiercely blue eyes was standing beside the table. Crooked in one arm, he held a bunch of crimson dahlias. The color was so pure, Duncan wanted to steal a flower and press the petals onto a page. It reminded him of another painting of Zeus his art teacher had shown him, one in which the god was not a bull but a swan. He was embracing a woman, wrapping his wings around her, and beneath their radiantly white bodies, one feathered, one not, lay a cloth the color of the dahlias.

"This is Frank Lustig," his father said. "Frank, my younger son, Duncan."

He was so used to the hastily concealed double take most people did on meeting him—his dark skin, his dark eyes—that he barely noticed it, but he did notice Frank's lack of hesitation as he set aside the dahlias and offered his hand. Did Karel's eyes have the same dark rim and flaring blue iris?

"Thank you for finding *my* younger son."

His voice was different, Duncan thought, each word bitten off, precisely. "Zoe, my sister, was the one who saw something through the hedge."

"And I want to thank her too. I am here on behalf of myself and my wife and, of course, Karel. I hope you will understand that he cannot come himself. He sends his gratitude." As he spoke, an earwig skittered out of a dahlia and came to a stop, tiny horns motionless, on the edge of the table. Another followed. Neither Frank nor his father noticed.

While his father made mugs of tea, Frank explained that he had grown up in a small town near Prague and moved to England eight years before with the help of his wife's family; two of her uncles had come to England in the 1930s. He ran a small building company with his cousin. Duncan offered his finger to the earwig. The earwig refused.

"Does Karel remember what happened?" his father asked.

"Yes, but we are not allowed to talk about it." At the hospital, Frank said, Karel had been about to tell them when his brother came into the room. "Karel started screaming. We didn't know he and Tomas had quarreled. Later he talked to the police, but to us, silence. Now he's home, there is this huge thing that none of us mentions."

He means the elephant in the room, Duncan thought.

"But he gave a description of the man?" his father said.

Frank nodded. "A police artist came to the hospital. Karel told him eyes like this, ears like that."

Duncan filed the information away to examine later: the police used artists.

Every night, Frank went on, Karel made him check the windows and doors. Ten minutes later, he checked them himself. "I've never hit another person in my life," Frank said, "but when we find this man, who made my son afraid, I will do my best to knock him down."

Duncan remembered that night when he had gone from window to window. He wanted to ask, Was Karel different in other ways too? Did he like different things to eat? How did he feel about the color red? About grass? Did he have bad dreams? Did he remember the bales? The swallows? Had he ever read *The Little Mermaid*? But his father was offering chocolate biscuits and saying he'd made a banister for a house Frank had built. While they talked about work, Duncan captured the first earwig under a glass and carried it outside. Bravely it darted away between towering blades of grass. Back inside, the second earwig was nowhere to be seen.

AT SUPPER MATTHEW WAS STILL out. Duncan watched Zoe's plump lower lip push forward as his father described Frank's visit. When he finished, she said, "May I be excused," and without waiting for a response stood up, carried her plate over to the dishwasher, and left the room. His parents exchanged a glance.

"My Greek class is going on a tour of the Ashmolean on Saturday," said his mother. "Would you like to come?"

"Yes, please." He was already planning to visit his favorite statues in the museum.

His father focused on his carrots and said he had to do an estimate for a pergola.

After supper, Duncan stopped outside Zoe's room. She had found the boy; Frank should have spoken to her, but no one was to blame. Before he could knock, she called out "Go away." He went to his room, wrote a note—*You are not an accident*—and, trusting her to understand, slid it under the door. One day, when the three of them were arguing, Zoe had said, "At least you know Mum and Dad chose you. Matthew and I are just accidents." Both Matthew and he had disagreed. Matthew said accidents mostly happened to unmarried people. He had said that if anyone was an accident, it was him. His parents didn't have a clue who they were choosing.

As he lay in bed, he could feel Zoe's dark mood swirling through the house. Perhaps that was why, when he finally slept, he had a vivid dream. He was downstairs, walking from room to room. Everything was the same, the sitting room, the parlor, but then, as he left the kitchen, there on his left was a door he had never seen before. He opened it and stepped into a beautiful, high-ceilinged room, filled with pearly light. The furnishings were simple: a long wooden table with chairs. On the walls hung several pictures, reproductions of paintings he loved. He sat down at the table. A heavy sheet of paper was waiting for him, and four perfectly sharpened pencils. Nearby sat a woman. He could not quite make out her features, but her skin was dark, like his; she too was waiting for him.

A cat, wailing in the garden, woke him. From the dark rectangle of his window he guessed that it was very early morning. He went downstairs and made his way from room to room, turning on lights, opening all the doors, even the cupboards. But none led to the beautiful room. Back in bed, he tried to reenter it through the only available doorway: sleep.

Seven

ZOE

AS SHE LAID her bike down on the grass, two rabbits darted for the safety of the hedge, white tails flicking. The bales were gone; the stubble, beneath windy skies, was a dull brown. Perhaps Karel, in his blue shirt and black shorts, had paused here, experiencing his first twinge of doubt. Most of the time, Zoe thought, we behave as if everyone is going to follow the rules. If a man appeared here now, say the man from the churchyard, what could she do but run? Or submit.

She spread out her poncho and sat down in the lee of the hedge, a few yards from where Karel had lain. She had never told anyone, not even Duncan, to whom she told most things, about these moments when she left her body. Even the word "moment" was wrong. She slipped between the teeth of time. She could still conjure what she recalled as the first occasion. She was sitting on the beach, looking at the waves, holding a piece of seaweed in one hand, a whelk in the other. Her parents thought she was sitting quietly for once, but she was hovering nearby. She could smell the salt air, see the waves glinting and the sand with its

Morse code of seaweed and shells, feel the sunlight but she was no longer tethered to a single source of sensation. Then she was back again. The whelk had left an oval mark on her palm.

She couldn't make it happen. Sometimes it didn't for months, and she worried she had lost the knack. Then she would leave again. Now she waited, hoping to catch some reverberation, however faint: an aftershock. Nothing. A rabbit. Nothing. After fifteen minutes she was bored, and cold, and entirely sure that she was not leaving her body today. Walking back to the gate, she saw a pale-green crayon lying in the grass.

DUNCAN WAS IN THE KITCHEN, eating toast glistening with plum jam, reading a book.

"You left this in the field," she said.

"Thanks." He set the crayon beside his plate.

"What were you doing there?" She wanted to be angry—why had he gone without telling her?—but as usual he had disarmed her.

"I just wanted to see it again." He held out half the toast, and she took a bite.

"Me too. It's weird that the police haven't found the man."

"Not really. They never figured out who broke the window in the school cloakroom, and that's in the middle of town."

"I thought being there I might"—she eyed the crayon—"sense something."

Duncan took a last bite and ran his finger round the rim of the plate. "Maybe too many things have happened in the field," he said. "Like this house. Think of all the people who lived here before us, and some of them must have died here, like Granny. Sometimes I think I hear her talking, but I can't make out the words. Do you ever hear her?"

"No." But as she went to make more toast, she recalled how once or twice, as she drifted into sleep, she had caught stray words and phrases wafting by. "Now you've told me," she said, "I'll listen harder."

THE NEXT TIME SHE WENT to Oxford, she looked not at shop windows but at men, those alone and those with women; in some ways it was easier when they were with women. Had one of them lured Karel into the field? Her eyes flicked over a man close to her father's age, a boy around Matthew's. Neither looked like a bad person, but what did a bad person look like? Her father's last apprentice, Freddy, had a nicely freckled face and whistled while he worked. But one day the police had arrived at the forge; Freddy had been borrowing her father's tools to steal scrap metal.

After an hour of circling the streets, she took refuge in the Covered Market. She bought a cup of hot chocolate and lingered near the stall to drink it. The man who'd been behind her in the queue stood a few yards away. He kept glancing over. She pretended not to notice while taking in his five o'clock shadow, his dark hair skimming the collar of his faded denim jacket. He was twenty. Maybe even twenty-five. When she left, he followed. She made it easy for him, stopping to look in the shop windows she had previously ignored, waiting for his reflection to join hers before she moved on. In front of a shoe shop, he finally spoke.

.

"You're a hot little thing, aren't you?" he said hoarsely.

Close up, in full daylight, she saw that his eyes were blood-shot, his nails arced with dirt, his clothes not faded but soiled. She ducked into the shop and tried on pairs of boots until it was time for the bus. Back in the street, she looked neither to right nor left but ran all the way to the station. Only as she was queuing to board the bus did she dare to glance around. Her gaze fell on another man: fair hair, slightly haggard, standing nearby. His gaze, quick, unsmiling, met hers.

Eight

MATTHEW

"WILL YOU MAKE us a sign?" he said. "We'll pay you the going rate."

He had been pleased when the idea came to him. Duncan
would feel appreciated, and the result would be much better than
anything he or Benjamin could do. They were setting up a table
outside the Co-op on Friday afternoon: ARE YOU PREPARED FOR
2000? HAVE YOU CHECKED YOUR LAWNMOWER?

"Tell me what you want to say," Duncan said. "Would you
like pictures as well?" He was standing at his noticeboard, rearranging various postcards. His room, as always, was the neat-
est in the house.

"Pictures would be great. Maybe some of the appliances we're
demonstrating?"

"Are things really going to fall apart on New Year's Eve?"

"No, it's a joke. Computers may go haywire, but staplers won't.
Can I see your new drawings?"

Duncan straightened one last card and pulled out his large

sketchbook. Setting it on the desk, he began to turn the pages. Here was his friend Will, his teacher Ms. Humphreys, the neighbor's cat, their father's workbench. He turned the page, and there was the boy, lying in the field. Matthew heard his own sharp intake of breath. Beside him, he felt Duncan waiting for his reaction. He leaned closer, examining the boy's quiet face, his bare bloody legs. The next page showed him from a distance, a small, prone figure with a bale in the background. Yes, Matthew thought, he did look peaceful. He was torn between wanting to study each drawing and wanting to turn to the next.

"I remembered where I saw him before," Duncan said. "Last spring I was waiting at the bus stop when he went by on his bike. He waved. I think he mistook me for someone else, but it made me feel better about things."

By "things," Matthew assumed Duncan meant how seldom he could answer the teachers' questions. While Matthew was usually in the top three in his class, and Zoe did well in subjects that interested her, his brother came twelfth, or fifteenth, except in art, but not because he was stupid. He had an amazing memory, and once he understood something—Euclidean geometry, how to parse a sentence, the way hydrogen and oxygen bonded, why the repeal of the Corn Laws mattered—he remembered it precisely. "I'm following," he had explained to Matthew, "but then the teacher says electrons orbit each other, and suddenly I'm picturing them instead of listening."

Matthew bent to examine a drawing of Karel's head, each eyelash distinct, each link in the silver chain vivid. "This is exactly how I remember him," he said.

Duncan walked over to the window seat. When he turned around, he was holding a long, straight knife with a wooden handle. Matthew recognized the carving knife that every month or two his mother or father wielded over a roast, and every five or six months his father took to the forge to sharpen.

"Last night," Duncan explained, "I stabbed my mattress, to see if I could."

Matthew had the same lurching feeling he'd had when Zoe asked if the man would have picked her up. "You're crazy," he said. Then, "So could you?"

"Sort of. People are always telling you to be careful of knives, as if they had a will of their own, but it's surprisingly hard to stab something. You've got to do it all at once, really wanting to." He held out the knife. "Have a go."

Matthew looked at his brother's smooth bed, his desk with the sketchpads and boxes of crayons, his easel standing near the window: everything orderly and harmonious. "Stabbing a mattress isn't the same as stabbing a person," he said. "If I could pull a lever that hurt someone far away, I'm pretty sure I could do that. But if I could see the person, then I know I couldn't." Although if the person was Claire's father, maybe he could.

"Do you remember when we went swimming with Grandpa, and he showed us his scar?"

Matthew nodded. "His bayonet wound. What is a bayonet anyway?"

"It's a blade you fasten on the end of your rifle so you can stab people who are too close to shoot. Did Grandpa ever say what happened to the German?"

"No." He had never thought about the German. "He probably killed him, but he wouldn't tell us that."

"Remember how the scar had a little lip, like a mouth?" Duncan ran his finger caressingly down the blue sheen of the blade.

And with that phrase, "a little lip," Matthew could see his grandfather wading across the swimming pool, the puckered purple scar visible above the waistband of his swimming trunks. "You should put that back in the kitchen," he said, pointing to the knife. "Mum might need it."

"Mum won't need it for ages," Duncan said. "You just don't want me to keep stabbing my mattress, like a mad person." But he carried the knife away.

That night when the house was quiet, Matthew padded downstairs and searched the kitchen drawers until he found the knife. In his room, he peeled back the sheets and tried to stab a corner of his mattress. He had been taking fencing lessons for two years, but lunging with a foil, at a masked opponent seven or eight feet away, was very different from the intimacy of a knife. The first few times his arm faltered; the blade barely pierced the mattress cover. He closed his eyes, counted to three, and plunged the blade into the springy innards.

Nine

ZOE

WHEN HER MOTHER announced that the detective was coming back to talk to them, her first thought was that they'd caught the man, but as soon as Hugh Price stepped into the kitchen, she knew they hadn't. Her mother offered tea, which he refused, and said she'd be upstairs.

"This shouldn't take long," he said. "Shall we sit down?"

Her brothers chose their normal places at the table; she chose her mother's, facing him.

"I wanted to tell you what we've learned so far," he said, "and to check whether you've remembered anything else."

Did it make sense, Zoe wondered, that they would remember more, not less, as the days passed?

He began by repeating what he'd told them on his first visit. Karel had finished his shift at the hospital only to discover that his bike had a flat tire. Typically he went straight home, but that morning he was meeting someone in their town. He decided to hitch. A few dozen cars passed, then a car pulled over. The driver, a man in his thirties, wore a suit. He was on his way to a meeting in Chipping Norton and would be happy to drop Karel off.

Glancing occasionally at his notes, the detective recounted their conversation. When Karel volunteered that he worked nights at the hospital, the man said he used to work as a night watchman in London. From eight p.m. to eight a.m. he had been alone in a building meant for a hundred people. Every night he was convinced that the world had ended. When his shift finished, he would step into a deserted street. Karel was saying sometimes he felt that way when the man swore—the car was overheating—and swerved into a gateway. He got out to check the boot and reappeared, holding two empty lemonade bottles. Maybe there was a water trough in the field? The man remembered seeing cows there last year.

Who remembers seeing cows? Zoe thought.

"As they stepped into the field," the detective went on, "some rabbits ran for cover. The man raised a bottle and pretended to shoot. Suddenly Karel was sure there was nothing wrong with the car. He wanted to bolt, but he hoped if he pretended all was well, it would be. The last thing he remembers is saying he'd go and flag down a car. We're asking everyone to look out for a blue car, with two doors and a bent aerial."

"Did he say what kind of blue?" Duncan leaned forward, his elbows on the table.

"Sky blue. Or maybe baby blue."

"There was a baby-blue car."

She recognized his meditative tone; he was seeing the car in his mind.

"When? Where?" Hugh Price had been sharing his attention between the three of them. Now he focused entirely on Duncan.

"When I went to get help. One of the cars that didn't stop."

"Do you remember anything else about it?"

Zoe started to protest—Duncan was only thirteen—but the detective held up his hand.

"It had a wonky radio antenna. The driver braked like he was going to stop. Then he kept going, as if he didn't like the look of me. There was a dent in the back bumper."

"Did you see the number plate?"

This was a stretch, even for Duncan, but, surprising her again, he nodded. "Yes, it began DUN, so of course I remembered. I can draw you a picture, if that's any use."

"That would be very useful. One more thing. You keep saying 'he.' Could you see the driver? Or did you assume it was a man?"

Once again Duncan's face turned inward, studying his memories. "I could sort of see him through the windscreen. He had brown hair and a white shirt. I felt awful for noticing when I was meant to be getting help."

"Don't feel awful. Would you be able to draw the car?"

While Duncan went to fetch his sketchpad, she watched the detective write a series of numbered notes.

"Why don't you ask the public for help?" said Matthew. "Offer a reward."

The detective made one more note. "We don't want to alert the perpetrator. We've contacted every garage within a radius of fifty miles about the car."

"So," Matthew persisted, "do you think the man would have picked up anybody who was hitching that morning, or did it have to be Karel? Perhaps he'd been watching him. Maybe he sneaked into the hospital car park and sabotaged his bike."

He's been thinking about this, Zoe thought.

"Are you interested in police work?" the detective said. "We always need recruits."

Looking both pleased and flustered, Matthew didn't seem to notice the detective's failure to answer his question. "I'm going to university," he said, "if I pass my exams."

"We're not prejudiced against higher education. I studied anthropology."

"But do you think he might be right?" Zoe urged. "That the man was stalking Karel?"

Hugh Price spread his hands; it was possible, he conceded, but not likely. "No one reported a man hanging around the hospital, and Karel said the car stopped only after it passed him. We haven't ruled anything out."

Duncan returned, carrying several sheets of paper. It was hard, he explained, to get the boxy shape of the car right; he couldn't remember the front bumper. The detective studied the sketches. Then he opened a folder and held out a drawing of a man looking straight at the viewer, wearing a shirt and tie. "Have you seen this man before?"

"Good drawing," Duncan said. "You can tell his eyes are blue and a little deep set, and he has the kind of hair that never stays neat."

"Do you know him? Does he look familiar?"

"I don't think so," Zoe said reluctantly. Matthew said the same.

"He looks like the milkman," Duncan volunteered. "Only older."

At once she saw that the man in the drawing had the same square face, the same low brow, as the man she sometimes met on summer mornings.

"Oddly," said the detective, "Karel's older brother is a milkman."

He sent Matthew to fetch their mother and, when she appeared, asked if he could take their fingerprints, to eliminate any possible confusion. He started with Duncan, then Zoe. She admired the detail that emerged from beneath each finger. These swirling lines would still be the same years from now, when she was thirty, even forty. She stepped back, ceding her place to Matthew, but the detective was putting the ink pad away.

As soon as the door closed, she turned on him. "Why didn't he take yours?"

"He already has them." He described how he'd gone back to the field, looking for clues, and found Karel's St. Christopher and—

"But how could you go without us?"

"Zoe," Duncan said, "I went. So did you."

It was true, she thought, they had all gone back. Finding Karel was like nothing else in their lives so far.

Ten

DUNCAN

DURING HIS BRIEF period as a Boy Scout, he had learned that the compass has thirty-two points. Now he could say with confidence that each person in his family was heading toward a different one. Matthew was spending hours with Rachel, who was pretty and principled, but not kind. Zoe was searching for something; she didn't seem to know what, or whom. His father was nicer when he was around, but he was around less. His mother, between her cases and her ancient Greek, was always busy. Several afternoons a week he opened the front door and entered an empty house. By mid-October he couldn't bear it.

He found his father standing on a chair in the sitting room, putting up a new curtain rod.

"We need a dog," he said.

"But after Arthur"—his father moved the bracket fractionally to the left—"you said you never wanted another dog."

"That was how I felt then. Now I feel differently."

He remembered every minute of the afternoon he had come home from school to find Arthur in his basket, refusing to go for a walk, or even to eat. He had sat beside him, stroking the smooth curve of his head, until Arthur was sleeping soundly. His father had promised to take him to the vet in the morning if he wasn't better. "But I bet he will be," he said. Duncan had gone to bed, reassured, and woken a few hours later in terror. In the kitchen he had known at once that Arthur was gone. He spent the rest of the night sitting beside him, drawing picture after picture. The next morning they had buried him under one of the laburnum trees, wrapped in his blanket.

"Let me get these screws in," his father said. The drill whirred three times. He got down from the chair, moved it to the other side of the window, and climbed up again. "Should we look for a dachshund?"

"No. That would make me miss Arthur even more."

On Sunday they drove to the animal rescue. Duncan had imagined it like an orphanage, barred windows, the dogs thin and miserable, the air rancid, but as soon as they came into the clean, bright room, he could tell the animals were well treated. Cats to the left, dogs to the right. Each was in its own pen, behind a grille, with a bed and toys and food and water. Each had a biography:

Charlie Boy likes children over five and regular walks.

Rita has retired from greyhound racing. She needs a large garden and a stable home.

Max gets nervous if people stare at him but is friendly.

Almost all the dogs came over to smile at Duncan; most of them stood on their hind legs. If only he could pat them, but every few yards there were signs about not touching. He walked around the U-shaped corridor, stopping at each pen, and back again. He wanted the lurcher, he wanted the terrier, he wanted the spaniel and the beagle. It would be awful to choose one and leave the others behind.

"We had a spaniel when I was your age," his father said, bending to gaze into a pen. "Daisy. I taught her to roll over, and to fetch Dad's slippers. Sometimes she'd meet me after school."

Duncan knew better than to ask what had happened to her. The same thing happened to all dogs. The spaniel's coat was brown with white markings, and she wagged her entire body, but in the next enclosure Rita, the greyhound, gazed at him soulfully. *I need you.* A few feet away, in the next pen, a dog with an odd, crumpled face stood on his hind legs. *Choose me, choose me.* After circling the room twice, he and his father agreed to return next week.

As they drove home, he asked if his father too, when he opened the front door, could tell if the house was empty.

"Sometimes," said his father. "But sometimes it turns out I'm wrong. You're upstairs drawing, or Matthew is listening to music. I remember after Dad died, our house seemed empty for months, even when we were all home. We were just pretending to be ourselves."

What did that mean? Duncan thought. He pictured his father and Granny wearing masks exactly like their faces, speaking in voices that were almost, but not quite, their own.

HE WAS LEAVING THE NEWSAGENTS, his new pencils paid for and in a bag, when he saw the card in the window: a drawing of a dog, black, with large eyes and large paws, nicely done by someone not particularly skilled. GOOD DOG FREE TO GOOD HOME. No phone number, but an address Duncan knew, not far away. He wrote the house number on the palm of his hand. As he walked down first one street, then another, he tried not to be hopeful. Who would get rid of a dog if it didn't have a problem? He wished he could put into words what he was looking for: not size or age or breed (apart from no Alsatians, no dachshunds) but some kind of emanation.

At the sight of the house he checked his palm, hoping he'd got the number wrong. The front garden was thick with weeds. Moss grew between the bricks around the door; pea-green curtains sagged in the windows. Remembering the drawing, Duncan pushed open the gate. The doorbell, when he pressed it, was dead. He knocked twice.

He was bending to move a snail off the path when he heard the latch turn. Two slender feet clad in black socks occupied the threshold. "Hey," said a voice. A boy, a little older than Matthew, was regarding him with an open gaze.

"Hey." He set the snail down among the weeds. "I saw your notice in the newsagents, about the 'good dog.' "

Something changed in the boy's expression; had the dog already gone? "I don't mean to be rude," he said, "but is this okay with your mum and dad? Not everyone likes dogs."

"It's definitely okay." He explained about Arthur and the failed visit to the animal rescue. "Why don't you want your dog any-more?"

"I'm going to London. I can't take care of Lily as well as my-self. She needs company, regular walks."

Lily, thought Duncan.

The boy opened the door wide and led the way down a cor-ridor. In the kitchen a black dog, bigger than Arthur, smaller than Leo, was sitting on a tattered red rug, her front paws, not especially large, neatly together. Duncan knelt down a couple of yards away and held out his hand. Her coat was sleek, like that of a black Labrador, but her ears were pricked, like those of a corgi, only smaller. She studied him for a few seconds. Then she stood up and walked toward him, taking him in with her dark eyes. She was not a puppy but still young. She sniffed his hand, sat down, and held up her right paw. The invitation was clear. He felt the rough pads, the prick of nails. Lily emanated.

"She likes you," said the boy. "And you seem to like her."

"How old is she?" He squeezed her paw gently and released it.

"I don't know. She's an orphan. One night last Christmas I came home and she was curled up on the doorstep, shivering. She was so small she'd squeezed under the garden gate. I brought her in and fed her, and in the morning I went up and down the street, asking if anyone had lost a puppy. I put up notices. No one re-sponded, so I decided she'd claimed me. Now she's claiming you."

He squatted down beside Duncan. Lily pressed her head against his knee. "I'd keep you if I could," he said. Her dark eyes under-stood and forgave. "Will you let me visit her?"

"Whenever you like. When can I take her?"

"Now. I'll walk with you to carry her basket. That way I'll know where you live."

Within a few minutes the boy had gathered up Lily's basket, her biscuits and tins of food, and a small stuffed bear. He put Lily on a lead and handed it to Duncan. The three of them walked together, Lily in the middle, separating to let other pedestrians pass. The boy asked about Arthur, about the rest of his family.

"They sound nice," he said. "I bet you'll be coming to London one of these days. Maybe we can share Lily."

They passed a pillar box in which Lily showed no interest. Then a deeply fascinating lamppost. Duncan asked why the boy was going to London.

"I want to be an actor. My parents don't think I'm good-looking enough, or funny enough, or anything enough. I didn't want to leave Lily with them. They think she's just a dog."

So that was why they had left so quickly: to avoid the parents. "Here we are," he said. "I'll write down my address and phone number."

He watched the boy take in the tightly pruned rosebushes, the clean windows, the front door painted ultramarine, not navy, last year. He set the basket on the pavement and knelt to talk to Lily one more time. Duncan turned away to give them privacy. On a page of his English notebook he wrote down his name, his address, his phone number, and underneath, *Lily's new human*. "Owner" seemed presumptuous. He tore out the page and, when the boy stood up, handed it to him.

"I don't know your name," he said.

"Gordon Enright, but I may change it for the stage. She has

supper around six, half a tin. She likes three walks a day and lots of conversation."

On the last sentence Gordon's voice broke. Before Duncan could promise to take good care of Lily, he was running down the street. She started after him and, at the end of her lead, stopped. They both stood, waiting, until Gordon was out of sight.

"I'm sorry," Duncan said. "Come on, Lily."

The hall smelled of potatoes baking and onions frying, two things she didn't eat but that, nonetheless, he hoped, would make her feel welcome. He bent down beside her. "We're going to meet my parents. Don't judge them by their first reactions. They loved Arthur, and they'll love you."

Still on the lead, keeping close to his side, Lily followed him into the kitchen. For once his parents were both present: his father chopping parsley, his mother stirring something. At the sound of footsteps, they turned toward the door.

"What's that?" said his mother.

"This is Lily, our new dog."

At the sound of her name, Lily sat down in her tidy fashion and studied his parents.

"But where on earth did you get her?" said his father. "We were going back to the animal rescue."

"From her owner, Gordon. He can't keep her anymore."

How could he pick up a strange dog? Did he even know what kind she was? What injections she'd had? What if she was rabid? Or vicious? During this inquisition, Lily eyed his parents calmly. Gradually they stopped hurling questions and approached. When she offered first his mother, then his father, a paw, Duncan knew she would prevail. He unclipped the lead, and she went to say hello to Zoe, who had been watching from the doorway. His sister succumbed immediately. Then Lily walked around the edge of the kitchen, stopping to examine the radiator and the ficus tree.

Could she smell Arthur? His biology teacher claimed that smells were how animals wrote letters. He imagined what Arthur might have written: *Dear future dog, these are good humans though supper is sometimes a little late.* His mother filled a bowl with water, his father moved a stool to make room for her basket, and he opened one of the tins Gordon had given him.

Eleven

ZOE

LAST MAY, A few weeks after the man appeared in the church-yard, she had started going out with Luke, who was, he told her on their first date, three hundred and eighty-three days older than her. They went to the cinema, bicycled to Blenheim Palace and Wychwood Forest, ran the games stall at the school fair, played Scrabble, experimented with his parents' collection of gin. She liked that he knew things—how fruit flies pass on ge-netic traits, that an underground fungus is the world's largest living organism—but he was oddly stupid about people. When she asked if he thought his parents still had sex, his mouth gaped as if she'd asked whether they flew around the chimney.

Anthony, also a year older, was at first an improvement. He could tell a joke so that people laughed, and he had a scooter. She liked the wind in her face, the way the familiar houses and hedges flashed by. He told her he'd slept with a girl he met on holiday in the Dordogne.

"What was it like?" she had asked.

"Let me show you." He slid his hand under her thigh.

"I don't want you to show me." She pretended her leg belonged to someone else. "I want you to tell me."

He clicked his teeth. "Awkward. Embarrassing. The opposite of boring. Way too fast. I don't think she liked it. I felt badly about that. The second time was better."

At least he didn't pretend it was utterly wonderful. "Where were you?"

"In a boat shed, behind a boat. Zoe, this is weird. I don't ask you about Luke."

"You can if you want. I'll tell you everything he told me about fruit flies."

He had fended off her questions, and she had fended off his hands. They had been seeing each other for nearly two months when a group of them went to the cinema. She and Ant sat in one row; Moira and some friends sat in the row in front. Even while Ant held her hand, she noticed how his eyes followed Moira. The next day, as she climbed onto his scooter after school, the words hopped out of her mouth: "Why do you always look at Moira?"

"I don't," he said. "You're just jealous."

Both the idea, and his smug satisfaction, were enraging. I don't want to see you again, she thought. What a nice sentence. If she hadn't needed a lift home, she would have jumped off the scooter and said it right then. As soon as they stopped outside her house, she did exactly that.

"Brhh." He clapped his hands. Inside his helmet, he hadn't heard.

"I don't want to see you again," she repeated.

Ant stopped clapping his hands. "Why not? We have a good time. Is there someone else you like?"

"No. But I don't like you enough."

He sat back on his seat. Beneath his helmet, his eyes hardened in a way that made clear his anger. "You're such a liar, Zoe. You pretend to know what you want, but you don't have a clue. You're just scared to sleep with me."

"I may not have a clue about most things, but I'm absolutely sure that the last thing I want to do is sleep with you." She removed her helmet and held it out to him, an empty shell.

As she stepped into the hall, she heard her parents' voices raised in consternation. In the kitchen she found them, and Duncan, bending over a small black dog. Lily, Duncan kept saying. Zoe could see at once that he was not going to give her up. If their parents banished her, he would sleep in the garden, pitch a tent in a field. But already the tide was turning. Their father was patting the dog. Their mother was asking what she ate.

Then Lily was walking toward her, her dark eyes doing something that was the opposite of Anthony's. As clearly as if she had spoken, Zoe heard the words: He wasn't worthy of you.

Twelve

MATTHEW

"YOU AND BENJAMIN know each other too well," the fencing coach declared. He paired Benjamin with Cally, who was shorter but faster. Matthew he put with Leon, who was tall and long-armed but had been fencing for only a few months. At first it was easy. Matthew scored three hits in a row. Then Leon scored a hit, and Matthew's foil clattered to the floor. Stupid, he thought as he bent to retrieve it.

"Sorry," said Leon even as the coach was calling, "Well done."

Matthew adjusted his grip, and raised his foil. "Engage."

He lunged. Leon, foil wavering, parried. As they advanced and retreated across the room, Matthew began to understand that it was Leon's very lack of grace, his awkward footwork, his faltering lunges that made it hard to anticipate his next move. He feinted for the chest and hit the shoulder. Or vice versa. Again and again Matthew was sure he was about to score, only to find his foil blocked

"It was weird," he told Rachel that evening. "Our coach is

always going on about posture and footwork, but Leon ignores all that. It was like we were really fighting." They were sitting on the sofa in her living room, fully dressed, ready to spring apart at her mother's return.

"I thought fencing was fighting," she said.

In the V of her blue sweater was the locket he'd given her for her birthday. Sliding his hand toward it, he explained that fencing wasn't just about hitting your opponent. "There are rules, like in tennis or cricket. You have to aim for the torso. You have to take turns."

"But, Matty"—she pulled away—"you have to know when to ignore the rules. That's why Greenpeace launched the *Rainbow Warrior*. The governments were ignoring international agreements, killing whales."

Before he could ask was it really the governments, they both heard a key in the lock.

HE WAS FILLING THE DAIRY section, a container of milk in each hand, when a voice said "Excuse me." A man, a boy, Matthew couldn't decide which, was standing a few feet away. He looked familiar, but after nearly two years of working at the Co-op, that was true of many people.

"Excuse me," he said again—he had a faint accent—"are you Matthew Lang?"

"Are you Tomas Lustig?"

Three days in a row he had set his alarm, hoping to catch the milkman, and on the third day encountered not the young man he'd glimpsed last month but a middle-aged stranger. Tomas was working a different route, the new milkman explained. He promised to let him know that Matthew Lang wanted to talk to him. "I work at the Co-op on Saturdays," Matthew had said.

Now, as he unthinkingly placed the milk on the shelf, he studied his visitor. Tomas off-duty looked strangely different. Perhaps it was his faded brown trousers with pockets halfway down the thighs, or his watchman's hat pulled so low that it squeezed his eyebrows closer to his blue eyes.

"Yes," said Tomas. "Why did—"

His question was lost as Mr. Stoughton, a regular customer, tapped his way over. "Matthew, how are the university applications going? I'd like some mature cheddar."

While Matthew offered the red, the white, the extra mature, and asked after Mr. Stoughton's dog, Tomas radiated impatience. As soon as Mr. Stoughton moved on to the cold meats, he said, "Why did you want to talk to me?"

"We found your brother in the field. I was wondering how he's doing? Have they caught the man?"

Tomas's eyebrows came even closer to his eyes, but already another customer was approaching the dairy case. "The Green Man at six," he said, and headed for the exit.

FOR THE REMAINDER OF HIS shift, as he restocked shelves and assisted customers and worked on the till and mopped the floor, Matthew thought about what he would ask Tomas. Perhaps, even without knowing it, Tomas held the clue to Karel's assailant. If only he could think of the right questions. When he stepped into the Green Man, the pub was just getting busy, people meeting each other after work, stopping for a pint on their way home. Tomas was already seated at a window table. As he waited to order a half of lager, Matthew studied him, unobserved. Even without his cap, he bore little resemblance to the boy in the field—his nose was broader, his eyes more deep-set—but what really distinguished him was the black cloud that hovered around him. Like Claire's father, Matthew thought.

He was still several yards from the table when Tomas caught sight of him and began to speak. "Was he in pain when you found him?"

Matthew set his lager on the table and sat down. He repeated what he'd told the detective: Karel had seemed peaceful.

"That's good. Very good." Tomas gave a soft whistle. "He looked peaceful at the hospital, until he saw me. Then he started screaming. Papa said it was the shock, that he was confused. Tomorrow he would remember I was his brother. But tomorrow made no difference."

He described how he'd bought some cheese scones, Karel's favorite, and waited until his parents left for work before letting himself into the house. "I called out, 'It's me, Tomas.' When I went into the sitting room, he was standing behind the sofa, holding an ashtray. I said his name. I held out the scones. He didn't speak, just raised the ashtray. I can't say it was the worst day of my life. That was the day he was hurt. But it was the second worst. He treats me as if I've done something terrible. Other people do too. Last week my fiancée said she didn't want to see me again."

What was surprising, Matthew thought, was that he had a fiancée in the first place. "Did Karel—" he started to ask, but Tomas broke in. "We have to find the man who hurt him. Then he will remember I'm his brother."

A cheer rose from the dartboard on the other side of the room. A girl had scored a bull's-eye, and her friends were applauding. Watching the jolly crowd, Matthew wondered why he was marooned on this island of unhappiness. Tomas knew no more than him, had no access to Karel. He edged his chair back from the table. "The police—" he began, but again Tomas interrupted.

"No," he said furiously. "They've moved on. But the man who hurt my brother is nearby. If he thinks he's safe, he'll let his guard down." He was frowning not only with his forehead and his mouth but with his entire face.

"Are you looking for him?" Matthew said, edging back a few more inches. "Do you have any clues?"

"I search all the time while I deliver milk. Now I plan to go street by street. I know the man looks a little like me. I know he has a blue car."

"Well." Matthew was on his feet. "Good luck."

"Wait." Tomas too was standing. "Why did you want to see me? Do you know something? These have been the worst weeks of my life. Karel won't speak to me. Sylvie won't speak to me. I say good morning, and my customers don't answer." He held out his empty hands. "I don't understand why I'm being punished."

For your Tomas-ness, Matthew thought.

But Tomas was still talking. "I was hoping," he said, "you might help me."

Thirteen

ZOE

WITH ITS ORIGINAL gold lettering, MacLeod & Son, above the door and its black-and-white-tiled entrance, the butcher's was one of the oldest shops in town. Zoe had not been inside for years, but save for the new display cases, it looked exactly as she remembered. She took a cautious breath. Despite the trays of chops and steaks, sausages and mince, the air smelled of nothing in particular. While the boy ahead of her bought a pound of sausages, she studied the scotch eggs, neatly coated in breadcrumbs.

"Hello, Zoe. How are you?" Like her father, Mr. MacLeod played for the town cricket team; his garden was a highlight of Garden Day.

"Hi. I saw your sign." She pointed as if he might have forgotten the Help Wanted sign in the window.

Mr. MacLeod stepped out from behind the counter—his apron was reassuringly white—and explained that he needed someone to work from eight to two on Saturdays, to help customers, and to clean and stock the cases. But what about her studies? Her parents?

"My brother has a job at the Co-op. They'll be fine. Can I fill out an application?"

He laughed. "I know who you are, Zoe Lang. Your gran used to work here. Why don't we try a couple of Saturdays? Tell your dad I'll see him at the Salon meeting on Thursday."

When she announced her job at supper, her mother's fork came to a standstill. "Darling," she said in her careful voice, "what about your exams?" Across the table, her father's forehead furrowed.

She marshaled her arguments: her birthday was in just over a fortnight; Matthew had started at the Co-op when he was sixteen; they were always saying she needed to learn to manage money. "And Mr. MacLeod said Granny used to work there," she added.

"But you don't eat meat," Matthew said. "Why would you want to work at a butcher's?"

"You don't eat everything you sell at the Co-op." Beneath the table Lily nudged her leg.

"Zoe," said her father, "last year you almost failed Latin. You need to focus on school."

Normally she would have protested: Who used Latin in ordinary life? She was good at the subjects that mattered. Now she only wanted them to agree. "I promise I'll do my homework. It's only six hours a week." She gazed at her parents imploringly, in turn. Which of them would yield first?

"Well," said her mother, "let's see how you manage for a week or two."

Before her father could disagree—he was still frowning—

she passed on Mr. MacLeod's message about the Salon meeting. It was Matthew who had proposed the old-fashioned name for the town's annual fundraiser. Each year the committee picked a theme for the Salon and everyone paid to attend, either as audience or performers. Last year people had reenacted scenes from famous films. Matthew and Benjamin had chosen the diner scene from *Five Easy Pieces*. Their parents had played the hero and heroine in *I Know Where I'm Going*. Zoe and Duncan had applauded.

After supper, as they did the washing-up, she suggested that the three of them make a pact not to lie for a week. She had been mulling the idea since Ant called her a liar. She expected Matthew to laugh, and say "Weird." Instead he looked up from the frying pan he was scrubbing and asked, "What counts as a lie? Mum's always talking about how easy it is to manipulate witnesses. If you ask how fast the car was going when it *hit* the wall, people say twenty miles per hour. If you ask how fast it was going when it *smashed* into the wall, they say forty-five."

"Those people don't know they're lying." Duncan dried a spatula. "It's more like they're color-blind."

"I'm not asking you to testify in court." She slid a plate into the dishwasher. "I'm suggesting we try not to tell deliberate lies."

"So"—Matthew rinsed the pan—"if Benjamin asks what I think of his new song, do I have to say I can't stand it? Or can I say I like 'Broken to the Bone' better? Both are true, but the first is truer."

"Isn't lying better than hurting Benjamin's feelings?" Duncan said.

They both looked at Zoe.

"How can you call yourselves friends," she said, "if you can't tell each other the truth?" Even as she spoke, she remembered telling Moira she looked fantastic in her new skirt.

BY MONDAY EVENING DUNCAN HAD declared a ban on questions. "If you ask a question," he said, "people ask one back. Then you're stuck."

Their pact was hardest for him, she thought, because he was the most truthful. "You don't have to do this," she said. "It's just something I need to prove to myself."

"I know that," he said, "but it's interesting. I can see why there are monks who never speak."

Zoe had already upset most of her friends when on Wednesday the biology teacher called her and Frances, who sat in the next desk, up to the front. With her fuchsia lipstick and sleek hair, Ms. Hailey was one of the few teachers it was easy to imagine having a life outside of school. "It's not surprising you both got the right answers," she said, looking from Zoe to Frances and back again, "but it seems very strange that you made the same mistakes."

"I wasn't copying," said Zoe. "May I be excused?"

At lunchtime neither Frances nor her friends would speak to her. Even Moira didn't understand. "You mean you told on Frances because of some stupid pact?"

"I didn't say anything about her."

By Thursday Matthew and Benjamin had argued about a point in fencing. Duncan had told Will that a TV program he liked was stupid. They agreed to abandon the pact.

"I don't believe anyone always tells the truth," said Duncan. "It's too hard."

The idea that everyone was lying some of the time made the world feel slippery and unsafe, but the experiment had worked. She knew now that Ant was wrong. She was just an ordinary liar, nothing special. Even Duncan had to make small adjustments in order not to be driven out of town.

The next day she discovered one of her father's adjustments. She was at the chemist's, buying shampoo, when the cashier asked if she'd collect Hal's photographs. She put the envelope in her bag and forgot about it until she came across it that evening. What impulse made her open it? The first photo was of a sunset over the sea; the second of a woman standing on the beach, laughing, her hair blowing in the wind, her jeans rolled up. The photographer's shadow lay at her feet. Zoe recognized the beach—it was in Wales, near the cottage they sometimes borrowed from friends—and she recognized the woman. One afternoon last spring, when she and Moira were shopping in Oxford, she had seen her leaving a café with her father. She was tall, as tall as Hal, wearing a black T-shirt with a pullover slung around her shoulders, jeans, and running shoes. She was saying something to him, smiling, and he was smiling back. She looks nice, Zoe had thought as she and Moira headed to the next shop, and thought no more about it. Her parents had lots of friends she hadn't met.

Now she recalled how back in September, before they saved the boy, her father had suggested going to Wales for the weekend. But her mother was busy, and she and her brothers had plans.

Finally he had packed some clothes, his book about clouds, and his camera, and gone on his own. He had returned, voluble and relaxed, on Sunday evening and made a delicious roast chicken. And all the time, she thought, he had been with another woman.

Across the hall Matthew's radio wailed; from downstairs came television voices. Her parents were watching a program about the Renaissance. She could interrupt some genial historian, gesturing at the frescoes in a Florentine church. "Look at this," she could say. Or she could leave the photographs on the kitchen counter. But as she flicked through the rest of the photos—mountains, clouds, a mug of coffee on a windowsill, clouds—she knew she would do neither. She had gone out with Ant for two months; still she'd been irked when, the week after she broke up with him, he had offered Moira a lift on his scooter. And irked, in a different way, when Moira refused. Her parents had been together for twenty years.

A new song, more melodious, came on the radio. Suddenly she stopped daydreaming and thought about her mother, the person who was sitting on the sofa downstairs, who worked hard, who wanted to be a good person, who loved walking and now ancient Greek and who, they all understood, despite her skilled job, her good salary, her gift for reasoning, depended on their father in hidden ways. If she found out . . . Even in her thoughts, Zoe could not finish the sentence. Moira and several other friends had parents who were divorced. They made having two bedrooms sound glamorous. Here, in her one bedroom, she thought her father hadn't just cheated; he had committed treason.

The next morning, she waited until he was alone in the kitchen.

"Hey, Dad"—she held out the envelope—"the woman at the chemist's gave me your photos."

"Thanks." He was drinking coffee, reading the paper. He opened the envelope absently, drew out the photographs, and quickly—she had put the woman on top—slid them back. "Tell your mother I forgot something at the forge," he said, and headed for the door.

Alone, she sat down in her father's chair; his coffee cup was half full, still hot. She imagined him wedging the photos behind a horseshoe, or a row of tattered account books. Then she was no longer in her body, no longer in the kitchen of her home, but in some other limitless space, where she could simultaneously appreciate the wrinkled apple in the fruit bowl, Lily's toy bear, the tea towels hanging limply on the radiator, the silvery drops of water in the sink, the leafy ficus in the corner, her father's absence. And, briefly, they were all connected.

Fourteen

DUNCAN

LILY MADE THINGS better—he could answer more of Ms. Humphreys's questions; the house didn't feel empty—but even she could not prevent his family members from traveling toward their separate destinations. Night after night he woke to find himself searching for the beautiful room. Once he was in the parlor, another time standing over Zoe's bed; happily, she did not wake. Before he went to nursery school his parents had told him that they were his parents, but that Betsy had not given birth to him. His birth mother was Turkish; she had given him up for adoption because she was young and poor. His birth father was unknown. Duncan had accepted these facts like a fairy tale in which he himself played a small part. Once upon a time there was a poor girl who had a baby boy. Then his parents came and found him. They brought him home when he was three days old, and he lived happily ever after. For years he had not thought about his first mother, but now he knew that when he sleepwalked, searching for the beautiful room, it was because she would be there, her skin the same color as his, her hands or her ears or her lower lip like his.

His mother was in her study, sitting at her L-shaped desk, leafing through a pile of pages. She did not look up as he and Lily settled themselves on the floor beneath the windowsill with its row of cacti. The oldest cactus was the same age as Matthew; each spring it produced half a dozen small, fat leaves, yellow green at first and then, within a month, dimming to the gray green of the main plant. When a person came too close, the plant shot tiny stingers to protect itself.

"I was wondering," he said, "if you had a photograph of my first mother."

"Me?"

Even as she spoke, he saw his question reach her. Still he explained, "Not you. The person who gave me to you."

She made a small sound as if his words had wedged themselves in her throat. "I don't."

"Do you know where she lives?"

She pushed the pages away and turned to face him. Her hair was pulled back, and he could see the delicate curve of her forehead. "When you were born, she was living in north London, but that was thirteen years ago, nearly fourteen. Why are you asking? Did something happen?"

He gazed at her, bewildered. Of course something had happened. They had found Karel in the field, his pale face and his scarlet legs. And that night he had seen his first mother in the garden. Beside him Lily gave a small sneeze: Careful.

"She's just a word," he said, "and it's your word. Everyone

else in my life I can picture even when they're dead—I can see Grandpa's scar, Granny's nose—but when I think about her, there's no picture. Zoe has your lower lip, your hands, and Matthew has Dad's hands. I don't have anyone's hands."

He watched as his mother's full lips, her large eyes, and thin eyebrows shifted between those emotions he could name—sadness, astonishment, fear—and those he couldn't. She stood up and came to sit on the floor beside him and Lily. "There are rules around adoption," she said. "I never actually met your birth mother. She gave you to an agency. They made sure Hal and I would be good parents."

His imagination had betrayed him. He had seen the two women bending over him, his first mother offering him to Betsy, but the agency could have picked two totally different people to be his parents.

"I'm sorry," his mother said. "She was only sixteen. She wanted to do what was best for you."

He buried his face in Lily's neck. Did she remember her mother, her siblings? When they met other dogs in the street, he could never predict her response. Some, black, close to her size, seemingly kindred spirits, she passed without a second glance; others, once a dalmatian, another time a border collie, she yearned after. If there was a logic to her affinities, he had yet to grasp it.

"Duncan," his mother was saying, "you're our son. We love you." She said other things, about families, about how they didn't mean to deny his heritage. Remember all those books they had given him about Turkey? The map of Turkey in his room. How—

"I want to find her." It was the single most valiant sentence he had ever uttered.

His mother stopped moving, stopped breathing. "Then what? You'd want to talk to her? Be part of her life?"

Lily put a paw on his thigh, and he heard the unspoken question: *Be her son, not mine?* But no, he wasn't going to be like the little mermaid who gives up her family for the oblivious prince. "I'd like to know what I got from her," he said, "and I'd like her to know that she made a good choice. Then we can both go on doing what we're doing."

Last month in an art supply shop he had picked up two tubes of oil paint and been amazed that one was much heavier than the other. The man behind the counter had explained that the weight of oil paints varied according to the pigments. Did he love some shades of red because they were heavier? He could not see his mother's face as she sat beside him, but he could feel little darts of emotion, flying in all directions.

"Duncan, think how much you've changed in the last five years, and how much you're going to change in the next five. Why not wait? There's always time to do this, but once you've taken certain steps, they can't be undone. She may be living in difficult circumstances. Or she may be a very different person from the one you've imagined. Hopefully she's got on with her life, found work she loves, a partner. After you were born— this must be hard to hear—she probably did her best to forget you."

It was hard. He did not want his first mother to think about him every day, or even every month, but he did want there to be a space in her brain where the absolute fact of his existence was safely lodged. "I just need to talk to her once," he said. "To know where she is and have a photo of her." He held up his left hand. "Promise."

His mother sighed, a long, slow, mournful exhalation. "You shouldn't promise," she said. "You don't know what you'll feel. I'll talk to Hal, but whatever we decide, there's a very good chance we may not be able to find her. London is a big city. She may have changed her name. And you need to think about Matthew and Zoe. This affects them too."

Matthew and Zoe! They leaped into his brain. With their taken-for-granted hands, would they understand his need to find the person from whom he inherited the color of his skin, or his love of red? "I'll think about them," he said. He stood up and his mother did too.

"Would it help if you had more friends who"—she made a groping gesture—"looked like you? Maybe we haven't worked hard enough to provide you with a community."

"I like the way my friends look," he said staunchly. "This isn't about knowing more Turkish people. I don't feel Turkish. I feel like everyone else, except when people stare at me. This is about finding one particular person with whom I have a particular relationship. I didn't want to have this idea. It hunted me down."

Lily nudged him: Hug her. He stepped forward, and his mother's arms were around him. He smelled a smell he couldn't describe but had known all his life, a smell that meant home, comfort, consolation, colors he loved, half-spoken sentences fully understood.

Fifteen

ZOE

AS SHE LEFT the bus station, Zoe could picture the woman in her black T-shirt, with her wide smile and tangled hair, but walking up George Street, turning onto the Cornmarket, passing so many people, so many women, the image grew less distinct. Lots of women had long brown hair; some were tall. Perhaps she had already passed her without noticing? A man and a woman strolled by, swinging a boy between them; the woman wore a green sari beneath her anorak. A crowd of teenagers from one of the language schools passed in a wave of Italian. Two women, laden with bags, hurried by. She was about to give up and head to the shopping center when she realized she was gazing into the eyes not of a woman but a man. He was walking toward her, not exactly smiling, waiting to see if she would notice him. She looked back, curious and unabashed. He had high cheekbones, a strong nose, fair skin. His mouth was framed by a neat beard, almost the same shade of light brown as the hair that sprang back from his forehead. His leather jacket was a darker brown. The pavement between them dwindled, disappeared. With the slightest nod of acknowledgment—yes, he had seen her—he was past.

She turned to watch him, hoping he too would look back. When he didn't, she began to follow him. As soon as she saw him turn up Broad Street, she turned up Ship Street—it ran parallel—and started running. Without crowds or traffic, she could sprint down the narrow street. Then she was turning left on Turl Street. She slowed to draw breath and smooth her hair.

He might have gone into a shop, or one of the colleges on the far side of Broad Street, but there he was, once again, walking toward her. She started walking too, slowly, wanting to make the moment last. She had taken half a dozen steps when his gaze again met hers. She saw the jolt of surprise, then his delighted smile. He stepped out of the stream of pedestrians. She followed. They were standing near the entrance to the Sheldonian Theatre. From atop the walls on either side a row of massive stone heads, Roman emperors, ignored them, staring out over the crowded street.

"Do I know you?" he said. His boots were dark brown and expensive looking.

She shook her head, tongue-tied, even as she registered the cliché. He was older, she thought—twenty-two? twenty-three? Or was that the beard? His upper teeth were very regular, his lower a little higgledy-piggledy.

"So why are you following me? Or should I say intercepting me?"

He was American. Maybe that explained the beard, and the boots. Zoe heard herself say, "You look like a painting in one of my brother's books." She could picture the long-faced saint in his purple robe, the twisted rocks in the background, but not the artist's name.

"If you make a habit of telling strange guys they look like paintings, you'll find yourself in more trouble than you ever dreamed of." He reached toward her, but his hand stopped short.

"What kind of trouble?" She kept her voice equally low.

He laughed. "I'm not going to tell you that. Go home before some big bad wolf finds you."

His lips, framed by his beard, were pale and smooth.

"You go home," she said, childishly. Before she knew what she was doing, she had turned and was running down the street, zigzagging through the crowds.

Sitting on the bus, she felt stupid. His warning was an overture, the first step in a dance. Why hadn't she answered in kind? They could have gone to a café. She tried to imagine the conversation they would have had, talking about the Bodleian Library or the Radcliffe Camera, and all the time, below the surface, talking about something else.

Sixteen

DUNCAN

LIKE A LIGHT flashing at the edge of his vision, he sensed danger. He had wanted to show Mr. Griffin the illustrations in *The Little Mermaid*, pictures he had loved for as long as he could remember. Now he worried that his teacher wouldn't appreciate her endless devotion to the handsome prince whose life she saves from shipwreck but who never knows she's saved him.

"Wasn't there a film?" Mr. Griffin said vaguely. The frontispiece showed the mermaid and her sisters tending their garden lined with scallop shells. He began to point out the many faults: their faces were boneless ovals, their hair rippled like a bad Botticelli painting. And the seahorses were a travesty. "They're actually quite ugly," he said, "warty, with huge eyes on stalks."

Mr. Griffin's own eyes bulged beneath bristling brows as if they were trying to grasp whatever they saw. This was his first job after art school, and the smell of cigarette smoke, other kinds too, clung to his clothing, mixed with the smell of paint. Sometimes he forgot to remove his bicycle clips. He spoke fiercely about the differences between art, which he worshipped, and craft, an admirable but lesser undertaking. "Pretty" was one of his worst insults. "Decorative" a close second.

Now Duncan studied the picture, trying to view it as a stranger rather than a lifelong friend. "I've never seen a seahorse," he said, "but I like how there are wispy ink marks and at the same time you can see mermaids and flowers and fish. That's what I want to do—to make pictures where a lot is left out but people fill in the details. How do I do that?"

"I wish I knew," Mr. Griffin said, and Duncan understood that he truly did. "All I can suggest is keep drawing, keep looking at paintings to see how the artist is using the space of the canvas, how the colors and the composition work together. Keep making your own paintings." He went over to the shelf of art books near his desk and pulled out a slender book with a white cover. "Let me know what you think. He leaves out a lot."

That evening Duncan found himself looking not at Leda and the Swan, or Europa and the Bull, paintings full of color and movement that told a story, but at five bottles, or flagons, or vases—he wasn't sure what to call them—each a different shape. He turned the page and there were the same five bottles, the tallest one on the left. And again, and again. The paintings were small and the colors were cool: grays, purples, ochers, many shades of white. Sometimes the bottles were so sharply specific, he could have gone into a shop and picked them out of a hundred others. Sometimes they were ghostly, almost irrelevant. Whoever painted these, thought Duncan, loved the bottles. He imagined them lined up on the table in his beautiful room. His mother had still not mentioned his first mother, but he knew she had spoken to his father; they both praised him at every opportunity.

The next day, during lunch hour, he knocked again on the art room door. When no one answered, he stepped inside, thinking he would set the book on one of the easels that circled the room, and revisit some of the most intriguing paintings. He was heading for the nearest easel when he spotted Mr. Griffin seated by an open window, eating a tuna fish sandwich, and smoking.

"Hello," he said quietly.

"Bloody hell!" Last year, when he started teaching at the school, Mr. Griffin had used the same swear words as Duncan's father, but someone had complained; now he said mostly comic things: "Gordon Bennett!" "Holy mackerel!"

"I did knock. You didn't notice."

"And you didn't notice that I'm holding a little white cylinder." He stubbed out the cigarette. "So what do you think of Mr. Morandi?"

Duncan searched for words to describe his journey with the five bottles. At first the paintings had struck him as simple, even a little dull. Then, as he kept looking, he had begun to understand how they both were, and were not, about the bottles. Sometimes—it was hard to judge in a reproduction—the brushwork seemed almost clumsy, yet the paintings were complete. "I really, really want to see these paintings," he said. "Is the painter still alive?"

"No. He died in the sixties, in Bologna, a city in northern Italy."

Setting aside his sandwich, Mr. Griffin reached for the book and began to turn the pages. Together they studied the bottles, remarking on the soft gray of this one, the neck of that, the choice of ground, the shadows.

"I like this one," said Mr. Griffin, his eyes bulging toward a painting in which the bottles almost vanished.

"Do you think we'd like it as much if we hadn't seen the others?"

"I don't know. And I don't know if that matters. Plenty of great painters work in series—the paintings are in conversation with each other, and with the viewer."

As Mr. Griffin spoke, the bell for afternoon class rang. He swore again, and seized the remains of his sandwich.

AT HOME, AFTER A QUICK walk, Duncan invited Lily to his room. Choosing a sketchpad and a soft pencil, he set out to draw her as if she were one of the five bottles. Normally she enjoyed posing, or at least sat docilely. Today he had barely begun when she stretched a hind leg. Then she shifted from haunch to haunch, scratched her belly, sneezed twice, and finally, without a glance in his direction, trotted out of the room. Alone Duncan studied his three attempts, each worse than its predecessor: the lines muddled, the proportions wrong. Sometimes he could fix a drawing, but there was nothing here to fix. He tore the worst of the three in half, enjoying the decisive sound of fibers parting.

Downstairs everyone else was sitting on the large green sofa, watching *University Challenge*; Zoe perched on the arm to make room for him. He almost never knew the answers, but he liked watching the faces of the contestants as they ransacked their brains. And he liked watching his family hurl their guesses at the screen. Zoe was the quickest, but often wrong. His mother was good on the ancient world and food. His father had surprising areas of knowledge—the deepest fjord in Norway, the economic theories of John Maynard Keynes, how the borders of Hungary had been redrawn after World War I—but was slower. Matthew was good on nineteenth- and early twentieth-century history, and sport. Why had the drawings failed? Duncan wondered. The problem wasn't, he knew, Lily's restlessness; it was his bad drawing that had made her restless. As he listened to a series of questions about early arctic exploration—Shackleton, dogs versus ponies—the answer came to him. Morandi had looked at the bottles, truly looked at them, giving his vision over to their slender forms rather than imposing himself on them; he had painted them over and over, until all that remained was their essence. I need to be patient, Duncan thought. Draw a paw, an ear, an eyebrow. Then I might end up in a totally different place.

"Who painted *The Arnolfini Portrait*?" asked the quiz master.

Suddenly he was shouting, "Van Eyck."

"Well done," said his mother.

"Brilliant," said his father.

Seventeen

ZOE

SHE HAD NOT planned to look for the American but, day after day, there he was in the middle of biology or Latin or running; his face appeared when she was brushing her hair, or peeling potatoes. She heard again the odd lilt of his voice: *More trouble than you ever dreamed of.* She asked Duncan about the painting he'd reminded her of—some saint in a rocky landscape—and Duncan pulled out one of his art books and opened it to a pale-faced Christ, wearing blue and purple robes, mountains writhing in the background. She carried the book back to her room, and that made things worse. There were the high cheekbones, the shapely mouth, the brown hair, though much longer. She remembered her mother saying, "You have the right to change your mind. Right up until the last moment. Beyond. Don't let embarrassment, or fear, stop you if you want to say no." But I want to say yes, she thought. That was the conundrum: How to say yes.

So on Sunday when her mother said she was meeting a friend in Oxford, she ran to change her sweater. As they headed out of town, past the church and the primary school, her mother talked about one of her clients. While burning his wife's underwear in the garden, he had accidentally set fire to a hundred-year-old holly tree.

"The more I listen to him rant," her mother said, "and read his wife's depositions, the more I realize I'll never know what went on between them. She claims ten years of bliss before he started to work late every night. He claims it was a mistake from day two. I keep thinking they could still be happy if they could let go of their anger, but it's as if they're on two trains speeding in opposite directions. Neither of them can get off."

Was her mother suggesting that feelings were optional? That one could pick and choose between, say, love and hate, boredom and pleasure? As they swerved to avoid the postman's red van, parked half on the verge, no house in sight, Zoe set aside the idea to examine later. "Did you have boyfriends before Dad?" she said.

At once she worried she had come too close to what she longed and dreaded to ask, but her mother, sounding pleased, was already saying, "Several." She described her sixth-form boyfriend, Kevin, who was brainy and funny, then a couple of boys at university. "I kept looking for someone with whom I could share everything: work, ideas, travel, books, music. When I first met Hal, he seemed too different—a blacksmith who'd been running his own business since he was sixteen."

"You and Dad share lots of things." She heard herself pleading.

"We do."

Was that all she was going to say? Zoe did not dare to press her. But a mile later, as they circled a roundabout, her mother continued, "And our differences are mostly for the good. I'm always preparing for disaster. Hal reminds me there are silver linings. How was the Latin test?"

In the car park she leaned over to kiss Zoe. "If you want a lift home, be here at five."

They headed in opposite directions. She doesn't know, Zoe thought, with a gust of relief. But almost immediately, as she turned into the street, relief turned to dismay. What did it mean that her father was lying every minute, and that her mother had no idea? Perhaps even now he was meeting the woman. And what was she, Zoe, doing walking the crowded streets on a raw November day, stupidly hoping to find one person, a man whose name she didn't even know, among so many? The pavement echoed under her new boots, the people she passed looked chilled, cramped, in their tiny lives, the blood inching through their veins. Litter rattled across the pavement; a beer can rolled in the gutter.

"Fifty pence for a cup of tea, love?"

A woman, seated on the steps of a bank, was holding out a paper cup. Her turquoise tracksuit, only a little ragged at the collar and cuffs, made her eyes look very blue. Zoe's hand closed around a fifty-pence piece. Before she could change her mind, she dropped the coin in the cup.

"God bless," said the woman.

Two minutes later there he was, coming out of a bookshop. It was incredible, and it was true. He was on the far side of High Street, walking with another man, deep in conversation. He wore the same leather jacket. His hands, accompanying his words, made neat, precise gestures. She darted across the street and fell in behind him and his companion.

"But the northern Catholics . . . ," the other man said.

They were, she guessed, heading for the station. At the idea of him boarding a train, she panicked. When there was a gap in the traffic, she repeated her trick of their first meeting: crossing the road, running ahead, and crossing back. As the distance dwindled, her pace slowed. Suppose, in the midst of conversation, he failed to notice her? Or, even worse, failed to recognize her? What had seemed impossible—he'd forgotten their meeting— was both possible and probable. Closer, closer, and still he was engrossed in conversation, his face turned toward his friend. *Look at me*, she cried silently.

He was almost at arm's length when his eyes, at last, met hers. "Hello," she said, stopping midstride.

"Hi." He stopped too. Pedestrians swerved around them on the narrow pavement. "This is my friend, Jerome."

Turning to Jerome, she said brightly, "I'm Zoe."

"Good to meet you." Jerome too was American, indeed more American: his skin tanned, his teeth very white and regular. "Sorry, I've got a train to catch."

She fell in beside them. Jerome was holding forth about Shake-speare, whom, he claimed, had become a secret Catholic during the years he'd spent in Lancashire. "It's in the plays," he said, "if you know where to look. One of these days, I bet they'll find proof."

"You could get Ladbrokes to offer you odds," Zoe suggested.

Jerome smiled. "That's one of your betting shops, isn't it?

Three to one I'm right. Excuse me, I'm going to jog the rest of the way." He hugged the man, threw another nice-to-meet-you at Zoe, and darted into the traffic with surprising agility. They stood watching as he zigzagged across the road, one hand raised in supplication to oncoming cars.

"Well." The American turned to her, shifting his backpack to the other shoulder.

"What's your name?"

"Rufus. As you can see, I didn't take your advice and go home."

What could she say? But he remembered; their meeting had left its mark. She sensed him wrestling with something, another commitment perhaps, and then deciding.

"Shall we get a nice British cup of tea, Zoe?"

"That would be lovely, Rufus."

As they started walking again, she was torn between wanting to know ordinary things—where did he come from? how old was he?—and wanting to keep their conversation on some other level where everything that mattered was unsaid. They passed a man walking a border terrier. Beside her Rufus was silent. I must say something, Zoe thought. Anything.

"Jerome should come back in the summer," she offered. "Last year one college did *The Tempest* beside a lake, and another did *A Midsummer Night's Dream* in the quad, at sunset."

"I've never dared tell him," Rufus said, "but I'm not a big fan of Shakespeare. It always sounds like the actors are speaking a foreign language."

She was still grappling with someone admitting to not liking

Shakespeare when he opened the door of a café. The waitress waved them to a corner table. He ordered tea for two. She watched the way his mouth moved, the way his eyes changed. His hands were pale, and his nails were broad and shapely, flatter than hers. Spatulate, she thought, was that the word? Suddenly she noticed that the waitresses were slowing, the customers silencing. She held on to the edge of the table. Stay, she begged. A low humming filled her ears. Then the wood was once more hard beneath her fingers; the bric-a-brac of conversation from nearby tables returned. He was watching her, eyebrows slightly raised. Had he noticed her tiny absence? The idea was both pleasing and terrifying.

He told her about Jerome. They had met at university. He was an amazing actor, had been onstage and in a TV series. Then he'd got involved in politics, writing speeches for a left-wing senator. When the senator lost his reelection, Jerome had returned to graduate school. He was working on Webster, the seventeenth-century dramatist.

Zoe had no opinion about Webster, but she liked that Rufus had a friend who was in acting and politics. "What about you?" she said.

He was doing his PhD in philosophy at the University of Chicago and had a scholarship to study at Oxford for a year. As an undergraduate, he had fallen in love with logic. Recently he'd gotten interested in causation. When the tea came, he said, "Do you even like tea?"

"Not much," she admitted.

"Oh, well"—he poured neatly—"all part of the adventure."

He added milk to her cup but not his. She didn't know anyone who took tea without milk. "So which college are you in?"

With a little jolt, she realized he had mistaken her for an undergraduate. "I'm finishing school," she said and, hoping to fend off more questions, asked what he thought of Oxford.

"Amazing," he said, "but not quite real." He had grown up in a town that was founded in 1850; now he slept in an eleventh-century manor house. "And then there are all the famous people who've lived here. Maybe you're used to that?"

She said she lived in a town outside Oxford. "Don't you have famous people in Chicago? What about Frank Lloyd Wright?" There'd been a question about him on *University Challenge* last week; her father had known the answer.

"We do, but it's a big city. I don't think I'm walking where Saul Bellow walked, or having a drink next to John Dewey. Here everything is so close. When I work at the Natural History Museum, I feel as if Darwin might be just around the corner."

"Do you want to be famous?"

He smiled, and she saw again his crowded lower teeth. "That's a very personal question. It's hard to imagine stadiums of people cheering for a philosopher. Jerome was famous for a few months. It didn't make him happy, but he said it was easier to get dates. What about you?"

Beneath his attentive gaze her mind feinted one way, then another. He was right; it was a very personal question, one she had no intention of answering. Instead she described a photo she'd seen of Keats's grave, how he had died thinking his life was writ on water.

"Poor Keats." He reached across the table and put his hand on hers. "It's great talking to you, Zoe, but I need to tell you, I'm not looking for a relationship."

Everything—the warmth of his hand, the intentness of his gaze, the way his mouth moved—contradicted his words. They had left the tea room, with its ferns and its bad watercolors, and climbed out onto a high ledge, overlooking a stormy sea. They were balancing on the ledge, side by side; they could jump; they could climb back inside; they could stay there. But whatever they did, they must do it together.

"So what are we going to do?" Perhaps if she sounded like him, calm, almost analytical, he wouldn't take his hand away.

"We're going to finish our tea, and then, if you've time, I'll introduce you to an old friend at the Ashmolean. After that I must head to the library, and you'll go home to your idyllic Cotswold village."

"It's not idyllic. My father's having an affair."

"Who isn't?" he said, sweeping aside her stunning revelation. He removed his hand, and she understood that their conversation had once again shifted gears. They began to talk about normal things. He'd been raised in Cedar Rapids, which was in the Midwest. His father worked in a tool and die making plant and thought his studies pointless. His two younger sisters both had sensible jobs. She described her father's forge. "But he gets upset if we don't study."

When their tea was gone, he paid the bill, leaving a pound tip, and they walked over to the museum. What did he mean by "an old friend"? she wondered. A statue of a philosopher? But he led her past the Greek statues, clothed and unclothed, to the Egyptian section.

"Zoe, meet Meresamun," he said. "Meresamun is a singer in the temple of Amun."

While she gazed at the mummy, he told her what he remembered from his tour of the museum. "The Egyptians believed you could only survive for eternity if your name was preserved. One part of the soul remained in the tomb and needed food and drink, entertainment. Another part traveled to the Field of Reeds."

Perhaps that was what had happened to the boy in the field, she thought; a part of him had already left and only later been persuaded to return. She leaned closer, studying Meresamun's bright blue eyes, the jackals below her collar. "I know you're not keen on Shakespeare," she said, "but can I ask you something?" She described Antony's final sea battle and how Cleopatra ordered her captains to desert him. "Why would she do that?"

On the other side of the case, Rufus too studied Meresamun. "Remember the day we met. Did you think if A then B, if B then C? Or did you just start running? Perhaps Cleopatra gave the order to her captains and only later understood what she'd done. Have you ever been in love?"

Several times, she wanted to say, but in the dimly lit room, bending over Meresamun, she confessed, "Not that I know of."

"Then the answer is probably no. I have, twice. You'll see it's very persuasive."

"And does it never last?" She wished she didn't sound so plaintive.

He laughed, but gently. "Everyone does their own research into that question."

Outside the museum, she thanked him for tea. "You're welcome, Zoe." He raised his hand. "Have a nice life, as they used to say."

He turned and walked quickly away. Look back, she implored, but he didn't. First one person then another hid him from view. He was gone. Oblivious to shops and people, she started walking to the bus station. She was rounding the last corner when someone called, "On your right." She turned to see her father's girlfriend pedaling past, a brown box balanced on her handlebars.

Eighteen

MATTHEW

ON HIS WAY to meet Tomas, he stopped at the library and asked if they had copies of the Bristol newspaper. The librarian brought him three months' worth. He started turning the pages, expecting at any moment to come across Claire's father, staring grimly at the camera, accused of hurting her or her sisters. But the few criminals pictured were younger men, guilty of bad behavior at football matches, or drunk driving. One stabbing. Three burglaries. After half an hour, the news blurring, he had to accept that his second encounter with violence, finding Karel in the field, signified nothing about his first. Setting aside the newspapers, he went back to the librarian's desk to ask if there was a list of car owners.

"Not that I'm aware of," she said, "although the police probably have one. If you know a person's name and roughly where they live, you might be able to find them on the electoral roll, but you'd have to go to the main library in Oxford."

He thanked her and headed out into the street. So much for his idea that he could sit at a desk and, Sherlock Holmes–like, track down Karel's assailant.

At the Green Man Tomas was already seated at the same window table. From the doorway, Matthew could see his slumped shoulders, his downturned mouth. He had heard Karel say only one word, seen him only unconscious, and yet he was sure that the boy in the field was utterly different from this hulking, gloomy person.

Lager in hand, he approached the table. "Hi," he said, pulling out a chair.

Tomas, in the way Matthew already thought of as typical, ignored his greeting and thrust a map across the table. "You take half the streets. I'll take the other."

The map was large scale. Matthew could see a black rectangle marking the school, another for the Cottage Hospital. "But how do we know he lives there?" he said. "That he wasn't coming from some other town? Wouldn't he be terrified of running into your brother?"

Tomas shook his head impatiently. "My brother said the man's breath smelled of coffee, and the car was still cold—he had not driven far when he gave Karel a lift. I think we should start with the area near the hospital."

Why hadn't Hugh Price mentioned the coffee? Surely that was a vital clue. "So what are you suggesting? We knock on doors, and when a man of roughly the right age and appearance answers, we say, 'Excuse me, where were you on the morning of Monday, September twentieth?'"

Catching the whiff of mockery, Tomas's dark eyebrows came even closer together. "We're collecting donations for Oxfam. I asked at the shop. If people have bigger things—sofas or chairs—they'll send a van. When there is a brown-haired man in his thirties, we check for the car. Your brother's description of the car is much clearer than my brother's of his attacker."

Matthew felt a little better, and a little worse. Collecting for Oxfam was a clever idea. Why hadn't he thought of it? "Have you told your brother you're looking?"

He saw that mentioning Karel was his most effective weapon. "Who knows what my brother knows?" Tomas said. "He is still pretending that I am the one who hurt him."

The door of the pub was opening and closing, opening and closing. His father's apprentice had joined a group of friends near the bar. Eileen, who sometimes worked the same shift at the Co-op, sat alone, doing a crossword puzzle. "You talk as if you have something to hide," Matthew said.

The corners of Tomas's mouth moved, slightly, toward the horizontal. "You are a good observer. I will tell you my not-so-guilty secret." One of his customers had a model train set in his garage. The morning Karel was attacked, Edwin had invited him to admire his new track. Nearly forty-five minutes had passed as the two of them sent the trains crisscrossing back and forth before Tomas remembered his duties.

Matthew thought of the sign he had seen at a railway crossing in France: *Un train peut en cacher un autre*. One train can hide another. "You should tell the detective," he said. "And your family. People think there's something you're not saying."

"The milk was only a little late."

"No one cares about the milk. People think you were sleeping with someone's wife. Or hurting someone."

A set of points shifted in Tomas's brain. "So if I tell Karel about the trains. Or"—he corrected himself—"Papa tells him, he would no longer think his mad thoughts?"

"Hopefully." Glancing down at the map, he saw that Tomas had divided the town into eight areas. "Do you really think he could be living so nearby?"

"The town has eighteen thousand people, maybe more. How many do you know? I live in a house with six flats and know none of my neighbors. Yes, I think this man lives here. I think perhaps he saw my brother around town. Karel is someone almost everyone looks at twice."

Matthew remembered his theory that the man had been stalking Karel. Which was more frightening: the random attacker, or the purposeful? Both, he thought, in different ways.

Nineteen

ZOE

WHEN SHE GOT home from the butcher's, her mother was circling the ficus with a watering can. Without looking up, she reached for a yellow leaf and said, "Can you take Duncan swimming?"

"Why can't Dad take him? I'm going round to Moira's."

At once she was dismayed—the last thing she wanted was to draw attention to her father's activities—but her mother, moving on to the ferns, said he was driving the fencing team to a competition. "I really need to do my Greek homework," she added. "It would be a big help, darling."

In her relief, Zoe said she would devote her afternoon to unpaid child care. Already she was looking forward to spending time with Duncan; perhaps she could tell him about Rufus. They gathered towels and costumes and emergency Kit-Kats. She brought her hair dryer in case the one at the pool was broken. Duncan stopped to say goodbye to Lily.

"Come on," she said. "We're going to miss the bus."

They ran down the rainy street, backpacks thudding. She let

Duncan set the pace until the last corner when, at the sight of the bus, lights glowing, she sprinted ahead. "My brother's just coming," she told the driver. As soon as he scrambled up the steps, the bus jerked forward. Duncan was smiling, and she could feel herself smiling too. If they'd left five minutes earlier, she thought, they'd have made it easily, but they wouldn't be so pleased. As she slid into an empty seat, she saw Ant ride by on his scooter. "There's Ant," she said.

"Do you miss him?" Duncan sat beside her.

"I miss his scooter."

"Now you have a job, you could save up to buy one."

"I'm only working six hours a week. Besides, Mum would have kittens." On her right shoulder she felt the chill of the window, on her left the warmth of Duncan.

"Do you ever wonder about my parents?" he said.

Did he somehow know about their father? Then, with a jolt, she heard the "my." He was asking not about Hal and Betsy but about those shadowy people whose DNA he shared. "No," she said.

"I've been wondering about them."

The bus thudded over the first of the speed bumps outside the primary school. "But you've never met them," she said. "They could be on this bus, and you wouldn't know."

He stood up to scan the other passengers. One or two people looked back, their attention caught by his serious gaze. He sat down again. "I don't think so. Put your hand on your knee."

She put the hand nearest him, her left, on her thigh, palm down. Duncan did the same. She saw her skin, that color called white, which in her case was some mixture of pink and beige, and her fingers, each a different length, the red tooth mark Leo had made, her nails a little ragged. Duncan's skin was closer to the color of tea without milk. His fingers were longer and thinner; there was a smear of blue paint on his index finger; his thumb was a different shape.

"So?" he prompted.

"Your birth mother was Turkish. She was living in London when she had you. That's all I know."

"What do you see when you look at your hand?"

"I wish I had longer fingers and could grow my nails."

"Your hands are the same as Mum's. Dad's and Matthew's hands are more like Granny's."

He was right. Narrowing her eyes, she saw her mother's hand, holding the steering wheel, pruning a rose, peeling an apple, writing Greek letters.

"How would you feel," Duncan said, "if I wanted to look for my first mother?"

She raised her eyes from their hands to his face. "Did something happen? I know Matthew and I sometimes give you a hard time, but we don't mean it. I thought Lily made things better."

"She does, but not everything. The night after we found the boy, I was looking out of my bedroom window, and I saw my first mother standing under the laburnum tree. I haven't thought about her in years, but there she was, in our garden. I mean," he added hastily, "not really. There were just trees, bushes, but there she was, in my head. Now she keeps coming back. Maybe I shouldn't look for her. That's what Mum thinks, not until I'm older. But what if I look in five years, and she's died? Or moved to Australia?"

That night she too had stood at her bedroom window, looking at the lighted windows and televisions of their neighbors flickering through the leaves. He's out there somewhere, she had thought, whoever hurt the boy in the field. "When I was younger," she said, "I used to fantasize about your mother. I thought she could be a brilliant artist, or a scientist, or a member of parliament. I'd look at women on TV, thinking they might be her."

To her left, she felt a chill; Duncan had shifted to the edge of the seat. His first mother was not hers to speculate about. "Sorry," she said.

They were passing sodden fields. In one a herd of black-and-white cows clustered around the gate, heads down. "So, you wouldn't mind," he said, "if I tried to find her? Mum said I should ask you and Matthew. That it's a family decision."

"How do you even start trying to find a person in London?"

"You're good at finding things. What would you do?"

His brown eyes were fixed on her. She had the piercing thought: I couldn't bear it if you stopped being my brother. "If you start looking for her," she said, "would you be able to stop? Or would you become obsessed, like one of those people trying to find the source of the Nile who goes on and on, even when there are lots of snakes and no water? If searching for her took over your life, that would be hard for the rest of us."

"I think I could stop, especially if you all asked me to."

He spoke slowly in the way he did when he was examining various possibilities. And then—it was just as Rufus had described, with nothing that resembled a decision, no if A, then B—she heard herself say, "We could look her up in the phone books at the library."

"You mean now? Without Mum and Dad?"

At once she understood the enormity of her suggestion. What if they opened a phone book and there, in the long columns of print, his mother was waiting? She started to say the library might not have the current London directories, but Duncan was already shaking his head; he'd think about it.

Swimming up and down the pool, her thoughts set free by the monotony of breaststroke, she considered various wretched possibilities. What if finding his mother changed Duncan? What if he wanted to live with her? Or what if—she remembered the woman in the turquoise tracksuit—his mother was living in dire poverty? Or had some awful illness? Or was a bad person? She imagined her parents struggling with requests for money, or help. How could they continue living in comfort, knowing that Duncan's mother was suffering? None of these, she knew, as she stared at the wavering blue floor tiles, were arguments she could make to Duncan. With one sentence about the phone books, she had almost wrecked everything.

In the changing room she took as long as possible. Wearing only her underwear, she dried her hair meticulously. Then she put on the rest of her clothes and applied mascara, trying to make each lash distinct. When she came into the reception area, Duncan was sitting beneath a poster of a woman doing the butterfly, her taut shoulders beaded with water.

"Do we have money for hot chocolate?" he said. "I don't want to go to the library. I need to talk to Mum and Matthew, and sort things out in my head. Is that okay?"

She put her hand on his shoulder to steady herself. "That's okay."

Outside the rain had stopped. Sunlight was bouncing off shop windows and car windscreens. Will and another boy from Duncan's class were walking on the other side of the street. They waved and he waved back. In the café they sat near the fire and studied the menu.

"I haven't seen you two in a while," said the waitress. "What can I get you?"

They both asked for hot chocolate.

"Did you get caught in the rain?" She nodded at Duncan's still-wet hair.

"A little bit. We were swimming."

"Good for you. Well, the sun's shining now."

"Wouldn't it be odd," he said when the waitress was out of hearing, "if there was no weather? What would we talk about?"

Slowly they were returning from the dangerous place she had taken them to. "At the equator the weather is all the same," she said, "but I bet people still find things to say: I saw a cloud last week. I think there was a breeze yesterday. Have you heard from Lily's owner?"

"Her former human. No. He said he'd visit when he was home for Christmas."

"I wonder if he got a part in a play. Is he good-looking?"

Duncan regarded her curiously. "I'm never sure I know what that means. Are Luke and Ant good-looking? Luke has more regular features, but Ant's face—the way he presses his lips together when he disagrees with you—is more interesting. Gordon has an interesting face. When he spoke, I could see his feelings. The house was horrible, and I think his parents were horrible too—he told me they didn't like Lily—but he seemed really nice."

"Maybe you could make a painting of her for him?"

"Whatever you did to your eyelashes makes your eyes look bigger. That's a good idea. You can talk to Mum about all this," he added, "if you need to."

Twenty

MATTHEW

HE WASN'T LYING, he told himself, when he said he was collecting for Oxfam, but as soon as his mother said "Good for you. Phone if you need a lift," he knew he was. As he practiced French conversation and discussed the origins of World War I, he imagined finding the man. At first glance, he'd be quite ordinary. He'd have taken off his suit jacket, replaced it with a sweater. He'd be drinking a beer, or a mug of tea. Then, as he began to talk, there'd be something strange about him. He wouldn't meet Matthew's eyes, or alternately, he'd stare at him fixedly; his hands would dart in and out of his pockets. What would he give to Oxfam? An old cardigan? A set of bowls?

How would Matthew know it was him? Perhaps he wouldn't. Then as he left, he'd notice a garage, or a wide gate across the driveway, and when he checked, quickly shining his torch, there would be the baby-blue car with the number plate beginning DUN. He wouldn't stop collecting, though; he'd knock at the next house and the next, finish the street so as not to arouse suspicion. Then he'd run to the nearest phone box to call Hugh Price.

Once again Tomas proved surprisingly well organized. He had a shopping cart and a roll of black rubbish bags. Matthew could put donations in the bags, and load them into the cart. When it got too full, he could leave the bags under the bench at the bus stop. Meanwhile Tomas would visit the more distant streets in his van. They would meet back at the bus stop at six-thirty. "Keep a list of houses where you get an answer," he said, sounding more like Matthew's manager at the Co-op than a fellow worker.

Almost immediately Matthew discovered that people were pleased to see him, and that most of those people were women. "Wait a minute," they said, and returned with a couple of sweaters, a tablecloth, a saucepan, a stack of books. "Thank you for doing this," said one. "Can you come back next week?" said another. The shopping cart filled rapidly. Twice he circled back to the bus shelter. Twice a Caucasian man of roughly the right age answered the door. The first spoke English with a strong French accent, and the second was so pleasant—he worked at a garden center. Would Oxfam like some trowels?—that Matthew discounted him. He saw no baby-blue cars of any kind.

By six thirty, when he returned to the bus stop, it was fully dark. Standing beneath the nearest streetlight, he leafed through one of the donated books: a photo essay of a safari park. He was eyeing a gleaming hippopotamus—Rachel had told him they were related to horses—when the van pulled up.

"Did you find anything?" Tomas said.

"Lots of good stuff." He gestured at the pile of bags. "Several people promised things for Thursday."

"But did you see a car? Did you see a man who seemed suspicious?"

"No."

"You remembered to look?" Tomas flung open the back doors of the van. "You did not get caught up in people's rubbish?"

"The stuff people gave me isn't rubbish," Matthew said indignantly. "It'll fetch decent money. I marked the houses where people want Oxfam to send a van, and those where no one was home."

"This is not about Oxfam." Tomas took a step toward him. "It's about my brother, and the man who hurt him."

Matthew stepped back, out of range. To his relief, two men were approaching on the far side of the street. He was not alone with this person who might fly apart at any moment. He wedged the safari book into his backpack, a gift for Rachel, picked up one of the bags, and carried it over to the van.

"I wouldn't be helping you," he said, "if it weren't for Oxfam. Did you find the car? The man?"

In the dim light he made out a mass of black bags filling the van. Despite himself, Tomas had collected an impressive number of donations. Matthew set his bag on top of the pile, where it slumped awkwardly. As he went to retrieve another bag, Tomas sank down in the back of the van. "I thought looking would bring us closer," he said. "But all these chats with stupid housewives, and we are just as far away."

After a school outing to see *Rosencrantz and Guildenstern Are Dead*, Matthew and Benjamin had spent an entire afternoon following the example of the two courtiers, tossing coins. He began to explain the gambler's fallacy. "Even if you get heads a hundred times in a row, the odds of getting tails the next time are still fifty-fifty."

"But we are not tossing coins," Tomas said. "We are knocking on doors, and there are a finite number. This man lives somewhere. I hoped we'd find a clue. That something, or someone, would tell us where to look next."

As they loaded the last of the bags into the van, Matthew thought he was right; the gambler's fallacy did not apply. He too had believed that if they knocked on enough doors, one was sure to yield the answer. Now he grasped the magnitude of their task. They were not two courtiers tossing a coin but two courtiers emptying a lake with a wineglass.

Twenty-one

DUNCAN

HE WATCHED HIS fingers playing "I Heard It Through the Grapevine" and tried to ignore the telephone directories, neatly stacked on the lowest shelf of the bookcase across the room. She wouldn't be in them, they were for Oxfordshire, but the three fat books, last year's, this year's, and the yellow pages, seemed to hum the question: Should he? Shouldn't he? In the swimming pool he had realized with a twinge of shame that the decision, for now, was moot; he did not know his first mother's name. His mother had told it to him only once, when he was three or four, not old enough to hang on to the strange syllables.

Mid-chord he stood up, went over to the bookcase, and pulled out the residential phone book for 1999. Column after column of names met his gaze. He turned to the Ls, and there, halfway down the first column, they were: Lang, Hal and Betsy. Then he looked up Will; his father *Henderson, Brian* was near the bottom. On the next page was *Humphreys, Eleanor*. Almost everyone he knew was included in these busy columns. He was searching for Mr. Griffin when he heard a soft thump at the door. Lily stepped into the room, circled the table, and stopped beside him. Bending to stroke her, he recalled Zoe's suggestion.

"Would it be okay if I painted your portrait? For Gordon."

This was a fine idea, Lily indicated, much better than moping over phone books.

In his bedroom she jumped onto the window seat and offered him a three-quarters view: black dog as figurehead. Duncan remembered his last disastrous attempt to draw her, when she had fidgeted her way off the page. Today Lily sat motionless while he pondered various decisions. Should she be at the center of the canvas? Should he include her surroundings, or any aspect of her life: black dog with red rose and glove? Then there was the challenge of her short, glossy fur, how to paint her so that she was both light and dark. He was drawing her ears when Matthew put his head round the door.

"Supper's ready," he said. "Nice picture."

Stepping back from his easel, Duncan decided to seize the moment. "There's something I need to tell you." While Matthew lingered in the doorway, he repeated what he had told Zoe, about his first mother appearing in the garden, his dreams of the beautiful room. "I want to look for her. Mum says I have to ask you and Zoe."

Matthew was pushing his hands through his hair, over and over, as if trying to push away Duncan's words. "But you're my brother. I can't imagine—"

"Suppertime," called Zoe from the kitchen.

At the table, his parents asked about his day. It had been quite ordinary—Mr. Griffin had shown them portraits by a painter named Lucien Freud; Will had a new calculator—but they kept saying "Well done" and "Great." Zoe didn't interrupt. Matthew didn't tease him. As his father said "Great" for the third time, Duncan understood: they were all afraid. Don't worry, he wanted to say. I'm just the same. But that wasn't entirely true.

He woke to find himself struggling with the French doors into the garden; beneath his bare feet the flagstone floor was frigid. Where was he trying to go on such a cold night? Gradually, in the almost darkness, the familiar room assembled: the fireplace, the sofa, the television, the armchairs and lamps and tables. He sat down in one of the armchairs and tried to sidle back into the dream. Once again, all the doors were closed.

He must perform three tasks.

1. Find out his first mother's name.
2. Finish Lily's portrait.
3. Meet with Karel.

Then he would know what to do.

Twenty-two

ZOE

YOU CAN TALK to Mum, Duncan had said, but the person she wanted to talk to was the American. She imagined them walking along the Oxford canal, or sitting in a café. He would listen, and then he would say something that made her stop worrying about her father's affair, Duncan's desire to find his first mother, Matthew's mysterious activities. Maybe afterward he would let her come back to his room. She pictured a narrow bed and a large desk. She wouldn't take off a single piece of clothing, not even her jacket, not even her shoes.

When she got home from the butcher's, her mother was on the phone, frowning slightly. Zoe guessed she was talking to her sister. She mouthed "Oxford," and her mother, covering the phone, said, "I think your father's going. Be home for supper."

Her father was in the parlor, typing invoices. She stood in the doorway, watching his nimble fingers. He was the fastest typist in the family, never looking at the keys, almost never making mistakes. As he typed, he gazed out of the window at the garden. They had changed the clocks last week; already the sun was closer to the rooftops. Was he daydreaming about the woman? Looking at the cirrus clouds and thinking of her hair?

"What's up, Zozo?" He turned to a new invoice.

"Mum says you're going to Oxford."

His fingers paused. "Yes, but I'm not sure what time I'm coming back. I might be meeting my friend Ralph, and . . ."

"Dad, don't worry. I can get the bus back." A few weeks ago, she might not have noticed his confusion; now it seemed blatant. They agreed to leave in ten minutes.

In her room she slipped a cowrie shell from her collection into her pocket and put on her silver earrings. She wondered if her father too would make special preparations, but he still wore his faded blue shirt, his worn jeans. "Don't let me forget to return my library books," he said as they pulled into the street. "Has Matthew finished his university applications?"

"Last week. He and Benjamin both put LSE as their top choice, and Sussex as their second. Did you ever think of going to university?" The possibility had only just occurred to her.

"All the time. When I was your age, I had my heart set on going to Cambridge. I wanted to be a surgeon. My father wanted that too. I used to help him on Friday afternoons and Saturdays, but he was always telling me to do my homework. 'You don't want to end up like me,' he used to say."

She pictured a TV surgeon, masked and gloved, holding a scalpel. Then she pictured her father, who could thread a needle, twist an iron bar, weld a hitch onto a tractor, glue a broken plate so that the cracks vanished. "I think you'd have been a good surgeon," she said. "What happened?"

He stared at the road ahead. "Dad went off to work on Monday morning, and dropped dead at his workbench. We had the funeral on Wednesday. On Thursday I was at the forge at seven, lighting the fire. Mum got a job at the butcher's—she'd be pleased you're following in her footsteps—and Joe did a paper round. It never occurred to us that we could have sold the forge, or leased it. At the time Mum was so broken by grief. Don't get me wrong, I like what I do, but when I chivvy you about schoolwork, it's because I want you to have the choices I didn't."

Was that why he saw the woman? He wanted a choice. His profile, clean shaven, gave nothing away. He braked for a cyclist and deliberately changed the subject. "So, we've decided about this year's Salon. We're calling it the Salon of Second Chances and asking people to dress up as the person, real or imaginary, they'd most like to be. Who would you come as?"

"Joan of Arc," she said, without thinking.

"Great. You can make your armor at the forge."

In Oxford she went first to the café where they had drunk tea. Two women, each with a round-headed baby on her lap, sat at their table, oblivious to its historic importance. Then she went to Blackwell's, which he had said was his favorite bookshop, but the many rooms, even the philosophy section, were filled with strangers. Back outside the shop, the only other place she could think to try was the Natural History Museum. Hadn't he mentioned working there?

She had last visited the museum on a school trip. Now, as the elegant facade came into view, her pace slowed. It was entirely possible, she thought, that she would live all her remaining days on the planet, however many or few there might be, without Rufus's company. She felt an unfamiliar pain beneath her rib cage. Inside the wooden door, a stuffed brown bear waited to greet her. She touched one of its paws for luck and stepped into the courtyard, with its vaulted glass ceiling, several stories high, a cross between a greenhouse and a railway station.

A group of tourists was gathered around the dodo display. Another group was studying a large skeleton, some kind of primitive lizard, its tail almost as long as its spine. On her last visit she had tried to draw it. Duncan had laughed at her attempt. She headed past the display cases to look through the doorway of the dimly lit Pitt Rivers Museum. Her father had told her that when the museums were built, people thought it important to keep the works of God—animals, plants, rocks—separate from the works of man—bows and arrows, masks, opium pipes, baskets. A dozen people were wandering among the shadowy vitrines, none of them him. Then she checked all four sides of the arcade that surrounded the courtyard. More people, not him.

Seized with the desire to know the worst—he was not here; it was over—she ran up the stone stairs to the first floor. A broad corridor, overlooking the courtyard on four sides, mirrored the arcade below. On the side nearest the stairs was a row of tables. Several were occupied by couples, families. The pain beneath her rib cage sharpened. Looking down into the courtyard, she saw that both groups of tourists had scattered. As she turned away, Rufus rose from a table at the far end.

"Give me a minute." He noted a couple of page numbers and put his books in his backpack. Then he was leading the way to

the stairs. On the top stair he kissed her cheek. "Thanks for finding me."

Briefly she put her hand on his arm. They descended the stairs
together. In the street the sun was shining beneath the clouds.
"Let's go for a walk," he said, and they headed down Parks Road.

"What were you working on at the museum?" she asked.

"One of those philosophical problems that will never be solved
about necessary and sufficient causes. I'm hoping it'll be part of
my dissertation."

"Does anything in philosophy get solved?" Beneath the plane
trees fallen leaves crackled underfoot.

"Some problems, in some areas—logic, math—but things
with solutions tend to stop being philosophy. I don't think we'll
ever finish discussing ideas of the self, or the problem of evil.
Maybe that's why the consolations of philosophy aren't very con-
soling."

He led the way down a narrow street and along a lane between
two buildings. As they reached Christchurch Meadow, a bell
chimed. "And there are always new ethical questions," he went
on. "Should the government be allowed to kill people, or make
them send their children to school, or have them vaccinated?"

"No," she said. "Yes, yes."

"So you believe in the law of excluded middle."

When she asked what that meant, he explained that either a
proposition was true, or its negation was true. There was nothing in between X and not X. They took the path across the grass
to the riverbank. Willow trees hung down. In the slow green

water two moorhens, red beaks bobbing, swam briskly; a male mallard followed, effortless and stately.

"Last year," she said, "we read a story about a town called Omelas. Everyone who lives there is happy. Then it turns out they're only happy because a few people are kept in a dungeon."

Why was she babbling about dungeons? But he was saying he knew the story; he'd given it to his students. "We had a really good discussion. Was it right to sacrifice a few people for the good of many? If so, who got to choose the scapegoats?"

Across thousands of miles they had already been thinking the same thoughts. "In the Bible," she offered, "it was the priest's job. He'd pick a goat, probably the oldest or the skinniest, and dump all the sins of the village on it. The villagers drove the goat into the desert."

"To starve, or be eaten by lions and jackals."

"Or live happily ever after, with the other scapegoats."

"A utopian community of scapegoats." He took her hand.

She was so amazed she wanted to shout. The path curved toward an enormous beech tree, its lower branches supported by stakes. When she could speak again, she told him about Duncan wanting to find his birth mother.

"I wonder why he suddenly wants to look for her?" Rufus said.

Fleetingly Zoe recalled the beautiful boy, bleeding in the field, but she was not ready, not yet, to break her promise to the detective. "I don't know."

A woman with two golden Labradors approached. "Good

afternoon," she said, addressing both of them as if their being together was perfectly natural.

"Hi," said Rufus.

"Good afternoon," said Zoe. Meeting the woman made her think of her father. Was he walking somewhere nearby, holding hands with the woman? What if they ran into him? But no, knowing she was in town, he would be hidden away in her flat, or some dusky pub. Still holding hands, she and Rufus stepped apart to avoid a puddle.

"I have to go soon," he said.

He did not say why; she did not ask.

They turned back. For a few minutes neither of them spoke. Around them the world fell silent: the sun sinking below the horizon, the clouds massing, the dark water flowing, the ducks swimming with invisible ease. "I hope your brother thinks things through," he said. "It's a big decision."

She confessed her suggestion about the phone book. "I feel like I handed him Pandora's box."

"But Pandora had no friends, and a terrible family. Of course she opened the box. We don't"—he squeezed her hand—"always have to act on information."

"I brought you something." Holding out the small pink shell, she explained that cowries used to be a form of currency. "I found it on the beach in Wales."

"Thank you." He cupped the shell in his palm, then put it in his wallet.

Before they parted at the gates of Christchurch, he wrote down the number at Holywell Manor, the place where he lived. Then he made her write down her address and phone number. "Don't worry," he said, seeing her expression. "I won't knock on your door."

"Or phone."

"Or phone," he repeated. "You can phone, and the porter will take a message."

We don't have to act on information, she thought as she walked away, but we nearly always do. Her hand, without his, felt empty.

Twenty-three

MATTHEW

BEFORE HE COULD protest—he was doing his homework—Zoe had crossed the room and was standing beside his desk. "I have to tell you something," she said. "You can't tell anyone, not Duncan, not Rachel. Not even Benjamin."

First Duncan, now her. "Benjamin won't tell if I tell him not to," he said, just to be annoying.

"Promise."

Sometimes, with her cynical remarks about Ant, her sharp insights into their teachers, Zoe seemed older, but the way she said "Promise," as if a single word could keep them safe, made her seem much younger. He put his hand on his French dictionary. "I promise I won't tell anyone. Not even Rachel, not even Benjamin."

"Dad's having an affair."

More than any evidence she might offer, his own immediate acceptance signaled the truth. What else made sense of their father so often being late, forgetting and muddling arrangements, of the way he had started seeing old friends and cooking new recipes with ginger and coriander?

Zoe was still watching, waiting for the effect of her words. "Aren't you surprised?"

"Yes, but not really. How did you find out?"

"I saw him leaving a café with a woman, and then there was a photograph of her on the beach in Wales. Remember the weekend he went to the cottage without us?"

He was nodding, rearranging the past. "And that day he was late to pick us up, the day we found the boy—maybe he was seeing her?"

They shared the satisfaction of solving a small mystery. Then Zoe, eyebrows arching, said, "Do you think we ought to do something?"

"Like what? Talk to him? Tell Mum?" He was throwing out suggestions, waiting to hear how they sounded.

"No!" she exclaimed. "He'd be furious if we said anything. We don't want him to feel he has to choose. As for Mum, I can't imagine what she'd do—drive the car into a ditch? Have a breakdown? I like living here, having two parents. You'll be off at university soon, but Duncan and I are stuck."

"You can always come and see me in London." Briefly, thinking of being at university, he felt better. Then the import of what she'd told him hit him. His father had put their family at the mercy of this woman; she could send an anonymous letter, or phone, or knock at their door, and everything would be over. "What do you think she wants?" he said.

Zoe fidgeted with her shirt cuffs. "She must know Dad's married, that we exist. Perhaps it's enough, their occasional dates. She looked like a nice person. She wasn't much younger than Mum, or tarty."

He had a sudden flash of himself and Rachel beneath her billowy duvet.

"When we found Karel," Zoe went on, "I kept thinking if I did, or said, the right thing, he'd wake up. Now I feel as if I'm waiting for someone, or something, to wake me up, but I don't want it to be Mum and Dad having a catastrophic row."

Alone again, studying the sentence he had begun—*Mon ami Benjamin n'aime pas*—Matthew thought, My family is in disarray.

FOR THE FIRST TIME HUGH Price had the five o'clock shadow of a TV detective, and his jacket was rumpled. They were in a small interview room, the ocher walls glossy and cracked, the only furniture a scarred wooden table with two chairs. He sat down in one chair, gestured to the other.

"Thanks for seeing me," Matthew said. "I was hoping you could give me advice." But he couldn't stop himself from asking first about Karel. Had they made an arrest? Did they have any leads?

"The case is still open. Maybe someone will spot the car." The detective tilted his head, as if hoping to see it in the distance. "Or the man will be caught for something else: shoplifting? speeding? Of all the crimes reported every year, I'm sorry to say, we're lucky to solve half of them."

Matthew had heard this statistic before. Now he thought what would it be like if his father bungled half his jobs, or his mother lost half her cases, or he gave half the customers at the Co-op the wrong change? Unzipping his jacket, he offered his sole morsel of information: the morning Karel was attacked, Tomas had been playing with trains.

"So he's a train junkie!" Hugh Price smiled his triangular smile. "How did you find out?"

He mumbled something about running into Tomas at the Co-op, how they had ended up collecting for Oxfam, keeping an eye out for the car. Across the table the detective registered every ounce of his confusion.

"Matthew, this man is violent, maybe a psychopath. You're a good-looking boy, around the same age as Karel. I can't stop you from collecting for Oxfam, but you and Tomas ought to stick together. No peering in garages, thinking you're Inspector Morse."

"Do you think he'll do it again?" The idea that he resembled Karel, even slightly, gave him a curious feeling.

"Probably not—all the evidence suggests a crime of passion—but we can't count on that." The detective pressed his hands together. "People talk about locked-room mysteries, but the ultimate locked room is another person's brain. What did you want my advice about?"

For a moment he was baffled. Then he remembered: Duncan. Did the detective have any suggestions about how to find his birth mother? He did. Telephone directories, the Turkish embassy, local papers, shops and newsagents, and if they could afford it, some private detectives were very effective. "Good luck," he said firmly.

Twenty-four

DUNCAN

AFTER THE FOURTH person asked, "Can I help you?" he understood that a dark-skinned boy loitering on a cold, damp afternoon outside a place occupied by the elderly and infirm was an object of suspicion. If the weather had been nice, he could have pretended to be sketching the Cottage Hospital with its many windows, or the view down the curving driveway to the street. As it was, he was simply standing near the front door, shifting from foot to foot, hoping to catch Karel as he left work. Reluctantly he abandoned his post and started walking down the drive. He was almost back at the street when a bicycle passed him. He didn't see the cyclist's face, only his dark jacket and dark jeans, but at once he was sure it was Karel. There must be a rack at the back of the building.

The next afternoon was even colder, even damper. He was walking up the driveway when the front door opened and a woman in uniform waved to him. He had no choice but to approach her.

"I saw you here yesterday," she said. "Are you looking for someone?"

She had gray hair and glasses and beautiful rosy cheeks and a chin that was negotiating between double and triple. All four made Duncan trust her, and wish he could draw her. "Sort of," he said. And then, as she kept watching him, not judging but simply waiting, he tried to explain. "I want to talk to someone who works here. I met him once, but he won't remember me."

"Do you know his name?"

"Karel. Karel Lustig."

Her features rearranged themselves. "How did you meet Karel?"

"I found him when he was hurt." Her gentle question made it seem all right to break his promise to the detective.

"Come." She reached out her hand as if he were much younger. He took it, and she led the way inside, down a corridor and into a small, plain room with a table and chairs, a sink and a kettle. A single picture, a misty street scene, hung on one wall. The woman pulled out a chair and offered him a towel and tea. He accepted the first, refused the second.

"I'm Hilda Epstein, the matron here. I want you to understand that Karel is an unusual person."

"Unusual how?" He already had his own answer.

"People tend to confide in him. And he's very truthful. Both make him vulnerable."

Duncan pondered this. "So working here must be hard?"

Hilda sighed quietly. "Truth to tell, I wish I'd never hired him.

Our elderly patients are all in love with him. They're convinced he makes them feel better, and I'm sure he does but their feelings are a burden to him. Whatever you say to him, he'll take to heart."

"I'm adopted." He had never said these words before.

Hilda's mild blue eyes regarded him steadily. "Do you have a nice family?"

"The best."

"Lucky you, and lucky them. I was in foster homes from the age of eight. People were very nice, but no one ever wanted to adopt me."

Her voice was not sad, nor was her face, but he sensed sadness. Whatever happens with my first mother, he thought, I'm never going to lose my family.

"None of this has to do with Karel," Hilda said, suddenly brisk. "He's back on days again, but he had to leave early. He'll be working his regular shift, seven to four, for the rest of the week."

"Thank you." He wanted to leave her with something, but what? He had come empty-handed, carrying only his schoolbooks. "Your patients are very lucky," he said.

From the slight flush that tinged her already rosy cheeks, he saw he had chosen the right gift.

THE NEXT DAY HE WAS at the bicycle rack at ten to four. Since his conversation with Hilda, his mind had been teeming with things he wanted to ask Karel. Had he known the three of them were there, in the field? Why did he say "Cowslip?" What was his favorite color? Did he get tired of the patients telling him things? What if you needed to do something that might hurt people you loved? What if just the idea of your doing it hurt them? The rack was at one end of the car park, in the shadow of a high, mossy wall. Standing beside it, he put all his energy into waiting. On the top of the wall a pair of wagtails bobbed back and forth; a small flock of sparrows scuffled in the ragged grass. The longer he stood, the closer the birds came. This is what it must be like to be a tree, he thought.

The back door opened. A woman walked over to the rack, unchained a bicycle, and without a glance in his direction pedaled away. The door opened again, and two figures appeared: one was not Karel, one was. Seeing him upright, walking, talking with another person, Duncan felt the ground shift. As Karel and the woman approached, the wagtails ran off; the sparrows rose, twittering, into the nearest bush.

"She's a hoot," said the woman. She was carrying the kind of black handbag Duncan associated with much older women.

"She makes everyone laugh," Karel agreed. "Except herself."

He did not have his father's accent, but his words had the same precision. He was tall, taller than Duncan had thought when he was lying down. The woman's footsteps were audible, not his. He wore a neat black jacket out of which his neck emerged, pale and slender. His hair was darker, but perhaps that was the gray afternoon; it was definitely longer. When they were almost at the rack, Duncan took a step forward. Neither of them noticed him. Then the woman did.

"Are you looking for someone?" Her voice, warm when she

spoke to Karel, was like a knife. As for Karel, his eyes darted in Duncan's direction, then focused on his bicycle lock.

"My name is Duncan Lang. I wanted to ask Karel a question. The matron knows I'm here."

"That's up to Karel." The woman was facing him, holding her handbag with both hands like a shield.

"Do I know you?" Karel was slowly turning the combination lock.

"Not really. I've met your dad. Could I walk with you?" Out of the corner of his eye he could see the woman still glaring at him. He tried to recover his tree-like stillness.

"For five minutes," Karel said. "Then I need to go home."

The woman took a step toward Duncan and threw a hard stare in his direction. *If you hurt this person*, she was saying, *I will never forgive you*. Turning back to Karel, she said, "You're sure you're okay?"

"I think so."

She continued to eye him for a few seconds before she unlocked her bike, wiped the seat, slipped her handbag onto the handlebars, and pedaled out of the car park. When she had turned the corner of the building, Duncan said, "I found you in the field. With my brother and sister."

Karel's eyes were like his father's: a dark rim circling tiny fractals of blue iris. Leaving his bike in the rack, he stepped over and, before Duncan understood what was happening, put his hands on Duncan's shoulders and kissed him, warmly, on each cheek. Then he stepped back and, for the first time, smiled. "You're younger than I imagined."

Oh, thought Duncan, I was already inside your head. Beneath Karel's jacket, he glimpsed the silver chain he'd seen that day in the field, and later drawn. "I'm thirteen. Does it hurt to remember what happened?"

"You're not reminding me. I'm always thinking about it. A part of me is still lying there."

"When we were kneeling beside you, you said 'Cowslip.' "

"Cow slip?"

"No. One word, like the flower. They're yellow. You see them in the spring. Shakespeare writes about them."

Karel blinked, neither claiming nor repudiating the flower.

They started walking, Karel pushing his bike—it made a slight clicking sound—Duncan beside him. Above the dark jacket a crescent of pale cheek was visible; on the handlebars Karel's hands reddened with cold. Step by step, in sideways glances, Duncan took him in. In his drawings, he thought, he had made his shoulders too narrow.

"That was what you wanted to ask me about," Karel said. "Flowers?"

They were walking beside another, lower wall. A snail in its topaz-colored shell was inching along the top, horns delicately extended. Duncan was eyeing it, trying to shape a sentence about his first mother, when Karel spoke again.

"I remember every minute of lying there. I have very thin eyelids. When I close my eyes, I can still see lights, shapes. In the field I could see birds and clouds. People visited me. People knelt beside me."

Duncan thought of the swallows darting overhead. Karel had

seen them too. The bike bumped over a tree root in the pavement.

"I thank you and your brother and sister for finding me. I am grateful, most grateful." *Click, click.* "But sometimes"—*click*—"I wish you hadn't."

The last words were spoken so softly, more like breath than sound, that Duncan wasn't sure he had heard them. Then, as Karel pedaled away, he knew he had.

Twenty-five

MATTHEW

IN THE CLOAKROOM they started talking about the millennium. Heather's mother, an accountant, claimed that everything was going to crash at midnight on December thirty-first. "But there must be safeguards," Matthew said. The idea of massive disruption was disturbing and thrilling: Big Ben with both hands stuck at twelve; trains running randomly; the Co-op giving out free food. Tim said there were safeguards, but some hacker in Moscow could topple the whole system. Raj said the important thing was not to fly on New Year's Eve. By the time Matthew collected his jacket and retrieved his books, the bus had left. He decided to visit Rachel. Between fencing lessons and his search with Tomas, they had scarcely seen each other for a fortnight. With luck, her mother would still be at work. He half walked, half ran through the darkening streets, knocked on her door, and stood back. Maybe he'd pretend to be collecting for Oxfam. The door opened.

"Hi, I was—"

Something was wrong. Her eyes were too wide, her mouth too tight. "Matthew, what are you doing here?"

His presence had never before needed explanation. "Can I come in?" He smiled, hoping she would do the same.

"Benjamin's here."

She could have added several things to that simple sentence. They were studying. He was borrowing a book. But none would have given more information than those two words and the way she stood, blocking the doorway. He turned and ran into the street. As he hurtled down the pavement, his footsteps drummed out the syllables: Ben-ja-min, Ben-ja-min. How could his friend do this? What had he done to deserve this? He took refuge in the bus shelter where, a week ago, he had stored donations for Oxfam. The bench was cold and damp; from the shadows beneath rose the smell of old chips. In the midst of trying not to shiver and trying not to breathe, he had one clear thought: he could not go to school tomorrow.

He didn't notice the car pulling up at the curb until the door opened. "Want a lift?" his father said. He settled gratefully into the odorless warmth. As they headed out of town, his father asked if something was wrong.

"I had a row with Rachel." Did two words count as a row? "We've broken up." He understood the cliché in a new way.

"I'm sorry. And right before Christmas, with lots of parties."

He hadn't thought about that. Night after night he, Benjamin, and Rachel would find themselves in dimly lit rooms filled with music and mutual friends.

"Breakups are hard," his father was saying. "Time is the only thing that helps. When I was your age . . ."

Suddenly he worried that his father might be about to confess his own romantic difficulties. Even in the midst of his misery he knew this must, at all costs, be avoided. As long as the woman was unspoken, she would have to be fitted into the small spaces left over from work and family. Any mention of her would be a step toward allowing her to take up more room. Desperately he began to talk.

"We didn't just break up. She was with Benjamin. We'd never have got together in the first place except for him. He was the one who told me to invite her to a film he knew she wanted to see. Who told me she was interested in recycling and stuff."

"Christ. No wonder you're gutted. Your girlfriend and your best friend. Are you sure? Benjamin's the last person I'd have expected to behave like this."

A dark shape scampered across the road, a vole or weasel dashing to safety. "They were there together," he said. "They wouldn't let me in. I keep telling myself that Rachel wasn't perfect. She went on and on about the Green Party, and a couple of times she wasn't nice to Duncan."

"People are allowed to be boring," his father said, "but everyone should be nice to Duncan. Sometimes when I'm about to lose my temper, I think, Could I tell Duncan what I'm about to say? Last week . . ."

He began to describe a client who kept changing his mind about a fire screen. Matthew managed to say just enough to keep the conversation going until they reached home.

LYING IN BED, HE PARSED the morning sounds—voices, doors, dishes, toilets—of which he was usually a part. He heard footsteps outside his room and a faint rustling. A sheet of paper slid under the door. A few minutes later, another followed. When the front door closed for the last time and his mother's car coughed to life, he retrieved the notes.

The first was from Zoe: *Hope you feel better. Let's plot RE-VENGE!!!*

The second from his mother: *Dear Matthew, there's soup on the stove, and the usual things for sandwiches. You need to go back to school tomorrow, so try to figure out what will make that bearable. See you this evening. Love, Mum. P.S. You're a star.*

Downstairs in the parlor he retrieved a cardboard box. He circled his room, gathering up reminders of Rachel: photographs, a cinema ticket, a scarf she'd knitted, prophetically already unraveling, a T-shirt from a concert, a note signed with kisses. He taped the box shut and wrote PRIVATE. DO NOT OPEN on the side. But where to put it? He couldn't bear the thought of it in his room, and Zoe, if she found it, would open it immediately. Finally he carried it to Duncan's room and pushed it under the bed.

When he woke again, his priorities were clear. The person he needed to talk to was Benjamin, his friend since their primary school teacher had put them in charge of the class begonia, his friend who had said *of course she likes you* and who had endured many afternoons of doing homework and hanging out with Rachel, his presence both superfluous and essential. And then, when Matthew and Rachel finally got together, his uncomplaining acceptance of their need for privacy. As for Rachel, he told himself firmly, she was pretty, she was good at chemistry, she had opinions, but within a hundred miles there must be a hundred similar girls. It was his liking that had made her special.

Could he hold on to this insight? Only, it turned out, for a few minutes. Then the noose of misery tightened again. He remembered her shyly showing him a new dress, paddling in the river on a rainy day. All those hours of talking, and doing it, were not going to vanish so easily.

Downstairs he made tea and toast and forced himself to contemplate tomorrow. He and Benjamin shared every class but one. Together they moved from history to French to algebra; later there was debating club and, on Thursday, fencing. He had never asked himself, Does Benjamin like me? Or do I like him? Their friendship was a given. As he showered and dressed and did homework, he clung fast to this thought. When Zoe came home, he asked her to phone him and arrange a meeting.

"The Green Man at six?" she suggested.

A pungent memory of Tomas made him say no, the Hare and Tortoise.

A few minutes later she was back; Benjamin would be there. Sitting cross-legged on the end of his bed, she said, "Are you going to have a fight? Whatever's going on with him and Rachel, it won't last. He's too clever, and too nice."

"He's not very nice at the moment. What makes you such an expert on romance?"

She pouted. "Statistically most teenage relationships don't

last. Unstatistically, Rachel has wandering hands. Remember Mr. Datta, the cricket coach last spring? She was all over him."

"You never told me that."

"I didn't want to make trouble. Besides, nothing happened. Were you really in love with her? I thought you just wanted to sleep with her."

Was that it? Had he only craved a few square inches of flesh? "Who cares?" he said. "The question is what am I going to say to Benjamin. He was there with her. They wouldn't let me in."

"I thought it was Rachel who wouldn't. Suppose"—Zoe clasped her hands—"he went round to her house to do homework, or play a new song. They were sitting on the sofa, and she—I don't know—put her hand on his thigh? Then you were at the door. Rachel liked the idea of two best friends quarreling over her, and pretended something momentous had happened."

He nodded slowly. Yes, he could imagine that. Benjamin carried away by singing, or solving a problem—both made him happy and heedless; Rachel taking advantage of him.

Outside the night was clear and frosty. He strode down the pavement, enjoying the cold air after being indoors all day, but as the pub sign came into view, the hare seated on the back of the tortoise, his knees threatened to buckle. He stopped beside a garden gate.

Could he do this?

No. No, he couldn't.

He was still standing there when he heard footsteps. "Cheers, mate," the jogger said as he pounded past. In his wake, a thought appeared in Matthew's brain: Who did Karel want to see so badly that even, after working all night and getting a flat tire, he had been determined to reach their town? In all his searching, he had never stopped to wonder. If he met Benjamin, he bargained, then he could go and ask Karel.

A couple of dozen people were scattered around the pub, but the only one he saw was Benjamin, seated at a table, two glasses of beer before him. At the sight of Matthew he half rose, his thigh catching the table; the glasses rocked perilously. "Hi," he said hoarsely.

Without looking at him, Matthew took off his jacket, slung it over the chair, and sat down.

Benjamin reached for his glass but his hand was trembling too hard to raise it. "I'm sorry," he said. "I screwed up."

He had run into Rachel leaving school. They had started chatting; she had invited him over to play his new song. He'd been sitting on the sofa, tuning his guitar, when she kissed him. "I swear, Matty, all I wanted was to get out of there. I knew she didn't fancy me. And then you rang the doorbell, and she did that thing. It happened so quickly. When she came back into the room, I yelled at her: Why hadn't she let you in? She said it was none of my business. I grabbed my guitar and ran all the way to the bus stop. You were getting into your dad's car and didn't hear me shout."

So Zoe was right. "Why did she want to break up with me?" he said. "Did she say?"

"I haven't a clue. You could ask her."

He shook his head vehemently. "If there's anything she wants to say, she can get in touch."

Benjamin at last raised his beer. "I feel like an idiot."

"Maybe she did fancy you for thirty seconds. It's not completely out of the question."

Watching him take in this small joke, Matthew remembered Duncan saying you could see what Benjamin would look like when he was older. "I don't think," he went on, "that either of us should be with Rachel. But if you told me you liked her, I'd have to understand."

Benjamin held up his hands. "I liked her because you liked her. I'm useless when it comes to girls. The ones I like never like me. I've only slept with one person." He gave a little shudder.

"I thought"—Matthew tried to sound suitably casual—"you'd never done it."

"Ages ago." Benjamin looked down at his beer, the foam thinning. "Before you and Rachel . . ." He did not finish the sentence, and Matthew understood: Benjamin hadn't wanted to leave him behind. "It was my brother's babysitter. One evening she was all over me. She was probably stoned. The next time I saw her, she told me to bugger off."

"You don't want to see Rachel again?"

"Not for one second. What we need to do is pass our exams and go traveling and go to uni. Then we can be in love, whatever that is. Or not."

"It's a plan." Matthew raised his glass. "Zoe asked if we were going to fight."

He spoke unthinkingly, part of the ordinary back-and-forth

of their friendship, but Benjamin's gaze sharpened. "That's not a bad idea," he said. "We have our foils, our masks."

"Maybe we could use the gym," Matthew suggested.

They looked at each other, appreciating the possibilities: a fight that was not a fight, as fake as Wallenia, or the broken corkscrews of New Year's Eve.

Twenty-six

ZOE

ZOE HAD THOUGHT she might need an excuse—returning a book, a tutorial—but the porter showed no hesitation in taking a message. *See you at the museum tomorrow 4 p.m.* There were only a few more weeks of term; then, except for her mornings at the butcher's, she was free until January. And now she was sixteen. Her age, which she'd so carefully concealed, was acceptable. She could leave home, she could have a lover, she could move to America.

"I'll tell him," said the porter.

She set to work on part two of her plan: how to spend the evening in town. Moira agreed to help in exchange for information. Her comments were painfully earthbound. "I thought you thought Americans were stupid." "He's so much older!" "You're not even interested in philosophy." But she agreed to go to an eight o'clock film; Zoe would be in the lobby at ten, and Moira's brother would give them a lift home.

At the museum she touched the bear for luck and climbed the stairs. He was sitting at the same table as before, not working but looking down into the courtyard. His face, unguarded, wore an expression of melancholy, like that of the saint in the painting. For a moment, she wondered what she had set in motion. Then he caught sight of her. He jumped up and kissed her.

"Here you are. I was afraid something had happened."

"I'm sorry I'm late. The bus met a herd of cows."

"You really do live in the English countryside."

As they walked down the street, he told her how the night before, a group of them had gone out to celebrate an acquaintance defending his thesis on Spinoza. They had just finished toasting him, when his girlfriend remarked that now maybe their sex life would improve. "You can imagine"—Rufus half smiled, half frowned—"we all rushed to change the subject."

Flustered by the phrase "sex life," trying not to show it, she asked what Spinoza would have thought. She could see he liked the question. He said he didn't think much was known about Spinoza's love life. He was Portuguese and Jewish and had lived in the Netherlands, where he made money grinding optical lenses. He had written about the work of Descartes and a huge, elusive book called *Ethics*, published posthumously. While he talked, Rufus led the way down first one street, then another. They were passing a graveyard, approaching Holywell Manor.

"I want to leave my bag," he said. "Then we can go for a walk."

She followed him through the doorway, across a small courtyard, and up three narrow flights of stone stairs. He unlocked a wooden door.

She stood there, taking in the room she had tried so often to imagine. The bed was under the slanting eaves, the desk, not as large as she'd expected, in the gable window. There was a small sofa with a lamp, and a coffee table. On the windowsill was a blue vase with a bunch of freesias. Had someone given them to him? A gray stone weighted a pile of papers. When she reached for it, the smooth oval exactly fitted her palm.

"A souvenir of the beach at Brighton," he said. "I've been here long enough to know I should offer you a cup of tea, but you don't like tea."

"No." She held out the stone. "My birthday was last week."

"We'll have to celebrate." He took the stone and gently replaced it.

"Maybe we could celebrate today?" She unzipped her jacket.

"Zoe." He unbuttoned his own jacket but did not remove it. "There are so many reasons we shouldn't do this. You're still at high school, I'll be going back to the States in June, your parents would be furious. Whatever we feel, having sex will, hopefully, make us feel more so."

He kept talking, at least his lips kept moving, but she had put her hands over her ears, replacing his words with the rush of blood. "I don't care, I don't care, I don't care. What are we alive for, if not to have feelings? I'll hate it when you leave, but I'll hate it even more if we're too cowardly to do anything. You said it's rare to feel anything; that when we do, we have a duty to pay attention."

He took her wrists, gently pulling her hands away. She glimpsed again that melancholy she had seen at the museum. "It's not that I don't want to, but—"

"I'm not a child. Mary, Queen of Scots was married by the

time she was my age." Nearby a door opened and closed; footsteps hurried down the stairs.

"But there are so many things," he said, "you don't know about me."

"Are you saying you don't want to sleep with me because I'm a virgin and don't understand causation?" It was the worst thing she could think of to say about either of them.

He started to laugh, stopped, and pulled her close. The knit of his sweater pressed against her cheek. She slid her arms beneath his jacket, feeling the hardness of his ribs, his vertebrae. "Quite the opposite," he said. "No, that's not right. I want to sleep with you because you're you."

He stepped back and, just as she was thinking he had changed his mind, began to kiss her. All her impatience vanished. She could have stood there for a year, two years. When, finally, he retreated to take off his jacket, she saw their two reflections in the dark window, almost touching.

"TELL ME SOMETHING YOU'VE NEVER told anyone," he said.

The light of the bedside lamp shadowed his face. "I used to think I could walk on water," she said, "if I tried hard enough." Then she told him about finding Karel in the field, although not what might have interested him most: namely that the events of that day had, somehow, led to the events of this one.

"So there's a person who wouldn't be alive," he said, "except for you."

"Have you ever saved anyone's life?"

"Not that I know of, although I do donate blood. Five years ago my father had an accident at the factory. Afterward he made us all promise to give blood when we were old enough."

"Tell me something *you've* never told anyone."

He breathed. She breathed. Some amount of time passed.

"When I was nine," he said, "a carnival came to a park near our house. I begged and begged and at last Mom said I could go with my friend Keith. She gave me ten dollars and told me not to spend it all at once. We went on a couple of rides. Then I wandered around. There was one stall where you had to throw a ball at a monkey; if you knocked its hat off, you won a prize. One of the prizes was a brown china bear, standing on its hind legs, holding a clock. Mom had said we needed a new clock, and this bear clock was the most wonderful thing I'd ever seen. I spent the rest of my money buying shots, and with my very last shot, the monkey's hat fell off. I was carrying the bear home, jubilant, when these older boys jumped out from behind a car. They just wanted to scare me, but I dropped the bear. It broke into a dozen pieces. I kicked them into the gutter and ran the rest of the way home. Mom scolded me for getting dirty."

"You didn't tell her what happened?"

"I didn't want her to be disappointed. She was so beautiful, and I loved the bear so much."

And me, she wanted to ask, am I beautiful? But he was saying something else, something that it took her a moment to understand: last year he had had a vasectomy. When he was seventeen, his girlfriend had got pregnant. Three agonizing weeks had passed before she decided to give up on marrying him and have an abortion.

"I never wanted to feel that way again," he said.

"So why did—" As the flow of their movements had grown most intense, he had reached for a small packet on the bedside table.

He pulled her closer so that his words tangled with her hair. "To be safe in another way. I think I'm all right—touch wood—but if anything happened to you, I would never forgive myself." She was still wondering if she had understood when he said, "I wouldn't have guessed you were a Scorpio."

"Is your birthday in November too?"

"April. I'm an Aries. Passionate and confident."

"I thought you believed in evidence and arguments."

He laughed. "Zoe, we wouldn't be here if I only paid attention to arguments."

Then his hands were moving across her body, suggesting they resume their deeply satisfying, deeply irrational activities.

Twenty-seven

DUNCAN

WHEN HE SAW the postcard of Big Ben by his plate, his first thought was: She found me. Somehow his first mother had known about his search and written to him. But on the other side was the neat printing he had last seen in the window of the newsagents.

"I didn't know you knew people in London," Zoe said.

She was at the sink, rinsing a glass. From the slant of her neck, the curve of her lips, he knew his sister had found what she was looking for. She had begun to treat her family with careless kindness. Then, as she filled the glass with water, he revised his thought: not what, whom. Only another person could have changed her so much. He pictured Europa riding Zeus. Don't let him carry you away, he begged.

"Gordon's coming back," he said. "He wants to visit Lily."

"That's nice," she said vaguely.

As he set the postcard on his bookshelf, he thought about London, the city where it had been purchased and written and posted and where, perhaps, his first mother still lived. He'd been there half a dozen times, most recently when Mr. Griffin had taken a group of them to the National Gallery and led them through five centuries of art at breakneck speed, holding forth in front of his favorite paintings—*A Satyr Mourning over a Nymph* by Cosimo, *The Ambassadors* by Holbein, *Whistlejacket* by Stubbs, *Saint George and the Dragon* by Uccello, *The Arnolfini Portrait* by Van Eyck—chivvying them past the bad ones. When they came out of the gallery, a band was playing gospel music in Trafalgar Square. Perhaps, Duncan thought now, his first mother had been there that day, dancing in the crowds.

He studied his portrait of Lily. He had tried first painting her on a solid ground, like Whistlejacket, Stubbs's famous horse, but that had made her look monolithic and, oddly, bad-tempered. Situating her in the garden seemed too random. Most recently he had painted her seated on the rug in front of the living-room fire. Granny's father had brought the rug home from India, and Duncan had spent hours lying there, reading. The soft greens and blues, with the occasional flashes of red and yellow, reminded him of the mermaids' garden beneath the sea. He set the picture on his easel and laid out his paints. Despite strenuous pleading, he was still confined to acrylics. All the paintings I love, he had told his parents, are made with oils. His mother argued that they were messy and expensive; his father, that the fumes shrank your brain. You're thinking of turpentine, Duncan had said. People use paint thinner now. They had promised him a set of oil paints for his next birthday.

As he flecked colors into the rug, trying to create the complicated greenness, he wondered if this was another mistake.

Would Lily appear to be floating on a magic carpet? What if he made the rug a single dark color: crimson? forest green? Then she would be sinking rather than floating. He thought again of Morandi's bottles. Perhaps what he needed was some additional element that interrupted the rug: a corner of the fireplace? a chair?

He went downstairs and studied the chairs at the kitchen table, plain wood with slightly curved legs, and in the parlor, straight legs with decorative knobs. He sketched both, shading them carefully with little pencil strokes. He had never noticed before that chairs, like people, have arms and legs.

TWO NIGHTS LATER HE WOKE with his hand in the knife drawer, and knew it was time to act. The next morning he waylaid his mother in the hall and asked for his first mother's name. "I've spoken to Matthew and Zoe," he said. "They understand." He stood waiting, pen and paper in hand, for the magical words.

But she was still moving toward the umbrella rack. "Duncan, I'm already late. Can we talk this evening?"

Before he could respond, she had chosen an umbrella and was gone. He felt a spark of anger—why hadn't she stopped to tell him?—and took refuge in a cherished image: a shimmering pyramid of eggs in a market in Bayonne. He remembered standing, watching the pyramid slowly dwindle as customers came and went. Maybe, when he finished painting Lily, he would attempt the eggs; he could imagine Morandi painting them.

That evening he was sketching the legs of a chair in the lower corner of the canvas when there was a knock at his door.

"You've captured Lily perfectly," his mother said.

"It's for Gordon, her former human."

"I'm sure he'll love it." Silent in purple socks, she approached. "She looks like she's about to smile. Your art teacher told us you're very gifted."

"Mr. Griffin? He never praises anyone."

She cocked her head like Zoe, although of course it was the other way round. "Well, he made an exception in your case. He told us that we ought to let you do art for as long as you want."

He was still struggling with the bewildering idea that they "let" him do art when he saw the sheet of paper in her hand. He reached for it.

"Duncan, you won't do anything without telling us?"

"No. I just want to know her name. It feels weird that I don't."

"Weird" stood in for the weightless feeling that had swept over him when he realized that her name wasn't in his brain; it seemed to reassure his mother. She let go of the paper and stepped back, watching as he took in the two words neatly printed at the top: *Esmeray Yildirim*. He sounded them out awkwardly, syllable by syllable, then repeated them, thinking even as he did so that perhaps his first mother said them in a totally different way.

"So I might have been Duncan Yildirim?"

"She probably wouldn't have named you Duncan."

"Do you think she did give me a name?" The idea that he might have another name filled him with amazement.

"She may have. Or she may have thought naming you would make giving you away even harder." There was a pause during which she kept looking at him, and he kept looking at *Esmeray Yildirim*. From the kitchen came his father's voice, calling "Betsy."

Alone he said the name ten times to be sure it was firmly back in his brain. Then he couldn't decide where to put the piece of paper. Should he pin it to his noticeboard? Put it under his pillow? Finally, he placed it between the pages of *The Little Mermaid*.

Twenty-eight

MATTHEW

ON MONDAY MORNING the corridors buzzed with the rumors Benjamin had started. Something was happening in the gym at lunchtime: a play? a fight? Matthew listened to the gossip, said "Wow" and "Brilliant." He could feel himself growing nervous. Coming out of history, he almost bumped into Rachel.

"Matthew?" she said, as if there were some question.

"Hi." In one quick glance he took in her smudged eyes, her rolled-up skirt, and kept walking. As he set his feet on one square of brown linoleum and then the next, he hoped she'd been impressed by his sangfroid. But if his blood were really cold, why was his heart pounding?

The gym was a long, two-storied space with windows on one side, wall bars on the other. Loops of rope hung down in graceful catenaries—Duncan had taught him the word—waiting to be released and climbed. At one end was a stage used for debates and school plays. He and Benjamin changed into their fencing clothes behind the curtain and stood listening while Hugo set up the boombox and organized the noisy crowd to stand on either side. When "Space Oddity" built to a crescendo, Benjamin slipped out of a side door and made his way down the corridor to the far end of the gym. The music stopped mid-chord; Matthew pulled down his mask and stepped through the curtains.

As he and Benjamin paced toward each other, he saw Duncan standing next to Will; Zoe and her friends were near the wall bars. He recognized almost everyone, and yet the familiar faces were transformed. His friends and acquaintances had become a crowd, hungry for spectacle. Ten paces apart, he and Benjamin stopped, bowed, and saluted.

"Engage," called Hugo, and they lunged forward.

Matthew aimed for Benjamin's shoulder, Benjamin went for his chest, Hugo called out the points. The crowd cheered, shouted. Suddenly Matthew's foil was flying through the air. He ran to retrieve it, ducking under Benjamin's thrust. They circled round, switching ends, pursuing each other up and down between the rows of onlookers. Several minutes sooner than they'd planned, Matthew lunged forward, flicked the foil out of Benjamin's hand, and hit him in the groin. In an instant Benjamin's white trousers flooded with red. He fell to the floor.

"Stop," cried a voice.

For one horrifying moment, seeing Duncan lying on the floor, Matthew thought that somehow, while pretending to stab Benjamin, he had stabbed his brother. He ran over and bent down beside him. Despite his dark skin, Duncan had turned remarkably pale. His eyelids were fluttering.

"Duncan, it's okay. Benjamin isn't hurt. Neither of us is hurt. It's just red paint."

"Cowslip."

THAT EVENING AT SUPPER, DUNCAN said he had an announcement to make. "I want to try to find my first mother, Esmeray Yildirim. I've thought about it, and thought about it. A part of me thinks Mum is right. I should wait until I'm older. But if I waited and found out something had happened to her, that I could have met her now, but I can't later, I'd be miserable. I know she might not want to hear from me, or she might not be a good person, or I might not find her, but I want to try."

He stopped, looking at each of them in turn, waiting for their response.

"But we'll still be your family?" said Zoe. "I'll still be your sister?"

"How could that change? You're the people I can draw in my sleep."

It was his fault, Matthew thought. The sight of Benjamin, covered in blood, had scared his brother into a decision. Reflected in the faces of his parents and his sister, he saw his own fears. All four of them wanted to stop Duncan from embarking on this search; all four of them knew that to let him glimpse their reluctance would be a profound unkindness.

"Of course we'll help you," said their father, "but there's a good chance we may not be able to find her. That you'll have to try again when you're older." Neither he nor their mother were eating.

"I understand," said Duncan. "I just want to do the obvious things—look in phone books, ask people. I'm not going to knock on every door in London."

Their mother explained that the agency wouldn't give them any information; it had been a closed adoption. "I'll ask my colleagues for suggestions," she said.

"Thanks," said Duncan. "It's hard for me too." As he spoke, his head dipped beneath the table. Lily must be standing guard.

And what would they do with his first mother, Matthew thought, if they found her? They could squeeze her in at the table, let her stay in his mother's study for a few nights, but could she really be a part of their lives? He tried—and failed—to picture an extra aunt, showing up on holidays, taking a special interest in Duncan. Between his father's girlfriend and his own imminent departure, there was already too much turmoil in the family. Half of all cases, he consoled himself, remain unsolved.

Twenty-nine

ZOE

SHE ANSWERED THE door, expecting someone collecting for charity or leafleting for a good cause, and discovered a boy, no collecting tin, no pamphlets, only a small backpack. He was smiling as if he already knew her; perhaps a friend of Matthew's? But as he started to speak, she heard the click of nails on the hall floor. Lily dashed past, a flash of black, and then she was pressing her head against the boy's leg and he had dropped his backpack and was kneeling, heedless of the damp ground, reaching for her, saying her name, burying his face in her neck. Gordon had come at last.

In the delight of their reunion Zoe forgot for several minutes about the cold night air. Then a car drove by, and she became aware that she was standing in the doorway, wasting the central heating, as her parents would say. "Come in," she said. "Duncan will want to see you." She headed for the stairs, trusting that one of them had heard her.

In his room Duncan was standing beside the bed, holding a

sheet of wrapping paper. When she described the stranger and how Lily had run to greet him, his lips parted in dismay.

"He's not meant to come until Christmas! What if he wants to take her away?"

Zoe considered the awful possibility—their home, Lily-less—but something about the way Gordon had greeted Lily made her certain this was just a visit. She said as much, but Duncan only looked more upset.

"It's so strange," he said. "I was just wrapping Lily's painting, to have it ready for him."

"That is strange," she agreed.

Downstairs Gordon and Lily were in the kitchen, sitting on the floor beside Lily's basket. At the sight of Zoe, Gordon jumped to his feet. As he introduced himself and apologized for showing up without warning, she saw why Duncan had said he had an interesting face.

"I'm Duncan's sister, Zoe. Would you like some tea, or something?"

He asked if they had Nescafé, and she found the jar of hardened crystals and filled the kettle. "How's London?" she said. "Duncan's coming."

"London is fantastic. I got a part." Smiling widely, he described how he was an understudy in a play; the day before one of the actors had sprained his ankle. "Now I get to be in three scenes. That's why I'm here. I don't have enough time off at Christmas."

In her relief she congratulated him exuberantly and asked about the play. It was set in a comprehensive school in Bradford.

"I kept going to auditions, and directors said I looked too young, or too nice. Most of the parts—"

"Have you come to take Lily away?" Duncan was standing in the doorway.

Gordon's smile vanished as he grasped the depths of her brother's fear. "No," he said. "She lives with you. I can tell you take really good care of her. Look how shiny her coat is. I'm just a friend who sometimes visits. Do you have a piece of paper?"

Duncan fetched the notepad that lay by the phone. Gordon sat down at the table, turned to a clean page, and, watched by Zoe, Duncan, and Lily, wrote several lines. He studied what he'd written, signed and dated it, carefully tore out the page, and handed it to Duncan. "Didn't you say your mum's a solicitor? Get her to keep this somewhere safe, in case I have an attack of amnesia."

Without reading it, Duncan folded the paper into his pocket. "I have a present for you." He set the parcel on the table. "I was wrapping it when you rang the doorbell."

Gordon did not remark upon the coincidence. Perhaps he was used to these kinds of things happening around Lily. He reached for the parcel and slowly, prolonging the pleasure, began to peel back the tape. When the picture came into view, he gazed at it in silence. Then his face broke into a brilliant smile. "This is the best present I've ever had." He jumped up, hugged Duncan, and bent down to show Lily the painting.

"Look, it's you. Aren't you gorgeous?"

Once or twice Zoe had seen Lily pause in front of the dark television screen, her head raised to study her reflection. Mirrors, mostly, she ignored. Now she wrinkled her nose, either at the smell of paint or at the image of herself, and took a step back. As for Gordon, Zoe could see how he would be onstage. She felt his delight as if it were her own. They were still debating Lily's response—Gordon claimed she loved it; Duncan said no, she was his harshest critic—when their father arrived home, and invited Gordon to stay for supper. Gordon asked if he might call his parents. As she laid the table, Zoe overheard him talking in the hall, his voice utterly different: flat and cold. She remembered Duncan saying the parents were horrible.

At dinner Gordon told stories about auditions and asked questions about Duncan's painting, the forge, her mother's ancient Greek. Her father described this year's Salon.

"Who would you come as?" said Duncan.

"Maybe Daniel Day Lewis," said Gordon. "Or Martin Sheen."

Throughout dinner, Lily sat at Gordon's feet. When he bent to say goodbye, she licked his hand and walked over to the French doors. He thanked everyone, put on his jacket, and picked up the painting, which Duncan had wrapped again.

"I'm going to hang it beside my bed," he said, "so I can see it first thing every morning."

Then he was gone and Lily was standing there, staring out into the dark garden. Duncan knelt beside her and read what Gordon had written on the sheet of paper. *I, Gordon Enright, do hereby give up all rights to Lily. I will never take her away from Duncan Lang and his family.*

No accident, Zoe thought, that Lily had chosen first Gordon, then her brother.

Thirty

MATTHEW

HIS OXFAM COLLECTING had taken him to parts of the town he had never seen before, but only after several wrong turns, and directions from two strangers, did he find the Lustigs' house on a street behind the laundry. He knocked twice and was still holding the dolphin knocker when he heard footsteps. A man with beautiful golden eyebrows opened the door. As soon as Matthew said his name, he reached out his hand.

"Thank you for what you did for Karel. Come in. Come in."

In the living room Mr. Lustig offered tea. Or beer.

"Beer, please."

He found himself sitting on a sofa, presumably the one behind which Karel had taken refuge, ready to throw an ashtray at his brother, and there on the coffee table was a marble ashtray. So Tomas did tell the truth sometimes. The room was surprisingly spare and modern compared to their sitting room at home, with its cozy inherited furniture. Here the armchairs and sofa were off-white, the tables and bookshelves made of light wood. Over the mantelpiece hung a painting of a castle on a hill beside a river.

Mr. Lustig returned carrying a tray with three glasses, three bottles of beer already bright with condensation, and a bowl of crisps. "Karel is coming. He works days now."

"Where is the castle?"

"In Prague. My wife and I grew up in a town thirty kilometers west of the city. We go back every summer. Our mothers are still alive, and many aunts and uncles and cousins. My aunt Vera painted that. For two weeks we eat big meals and walk by the river. We have a good life here, but there are only the four of us."

Would his father say that to a stranger? Matthew thought. *There are only the five of us. We have a good life*. Probably not these days. "Does Tomas go with you?"

"You know my older son." Mr. Lustig, reaching for another crisp, paused.

"We ran into each other at the pub. He used to deliver our milk."

"How is he? We do not often see him these days."

Matthew set his glass beside the ashtray. "He seemed"— angry? mad?—"out of sorts."

Mr. Lustig nodded. "I would have to agree. Did he give a reason for his out-of-sorts-ness?"

Matthew was still groping for an answer when, through the door, came the boy in the field. The shock of his appearance, both strange and familiar, propelled Matthew to his feet. He stepped forward uncertainly and was embraced warmly.

"Thank you for finding me." Karel took the other armchair. "You don't look like your brother."

"You know Duncan?"

"He came to meet me one day at the hospital. He was very kind."

Matthew could feel himself staring at Karel as if he were still lying, unconscious, in the field. His dark eyelashes made his eyes look very blue.

"So you know Matthew's brother, and he knows yours," said Mr. Lustig.

"I don't really know Tomas," Matthew said hastily. "We were both collecting for Oxfam."

He was wondering how to get Karel alone when Mr. Lustig said he must get back to making supper. In the wake of his father's departure, Karel seemed to forget about conversation; he gazed pensively at his untouched beer. Hugh Price was right, Matthew thought. The real locked room was another person's brain. "May I ask you a question?" he said.

Karel raised his eyes. "Of course."

"That day we found you, where were you going at seven in the morning? It must have been important, after working all night and getting a flat tire."

Most people received a question not just with their ears but with their bodies. Some slight adjustment of head or shoulders or knees showed that the words had reached them. Karel sat motionless. Could he somehow not have heard? Matthew was about to say sorry, it was none of his business, when he at last began to speak.

"I will tell you," he said, "but you must not tell Tomas. For three years my brother has been going out with a very nice girl, Sylvie. Last spring, they got engaged and we were all happy.

Then in August Sylvie's mother was admitted to the Cottage Hospital. She has diabetes, ulcers, many problems. Sylvie came to see her most days. When I had time, I brought her a cup of tea. I was being friendly to my brother's girlfriend. One day, while the three of us were chatting, Yvonne, she is the hospital cook, came to check on Mrs. Fletcher's diet. Afterward she said, 'That girl likes you.' I started to notice how Sylvie kept smiling at me, how she spoke mostly to me, not her mother. I asked Matron if I could go on nights for a month. My second week, Sylvie's mother gave me a note. Sylvie needed to see me."

His eyes met Matthew's. "I didn't know what to do. Yvonne said I must tell her I wasn't interested. We arranged to meet one morning after I finished work. We chose the churchyard to avoid my brother on his milk round. She thanked me for taking good care of her mother and began to talk about wanting to see Prague. It started to rain, and we had to leave."

He let out his breath in a sigh, quite different from the sigh he had given in the field.

"I hoped she'd understood, but her mother gave me another note. This time I practiced what to say with Yvonne. Three days before we were going to meet, something terrible happened. My brother was doing an errand near the hospital, and he visited Mrs. Fletcher. I woke up with his hands around my neck. When he let me speak, I said of course Sylvie and I were friends; she was his fiancée. But I could see he didn't believe me. As soon as he left, I phoned Sylvie. Her father took a message. I was going to meet her when the man picked me up."

"And then she broke up with Tomas?"

"She told him she never wanted to see him again. She swears she didn't mention me, but he suspects more than ever."

"So when he brought you scones, you were protecting yourself with the ashtray?"

Karel raised his eyebrows. "Tomas told you this?"

Matthew explained about their search. "If he finds the man, he thinks you'll forgive him, and Sylvie will take him back." From the kitchen came the clang of a saucepan. "Is there anything else you remember about the man? Any little thing that might help to find him?"

"I can tell you what his left earlobe was like, his left hand. Would that help?"

Footsteps, a radio. Quickly Matthew said, "In the field you said 'Coward.'"

Karel sighed again. "I probably meant myself. At the hospital I sometimes keep people company as they transition. That's Matron's word, not mine. They are on a journey with delays and reversals and a final destination."

He broke off, staring at the ashtray. Matthew gazed at him wonderingly. This boy had seen people die, had himself nearly died; he was the opposite of a coward. But even to say that seemed like another thing Karel would have to bear. A sizzling sound came from the kitchen.

"Now I try not to go out alone after dark," Karel continued. "If a strange man speaks to me, I jump. I keep hoping they will catch him and I will feel safe again."

Matthew had so many questions; one was pressing. "Why is Tomas so different?" he said.

"My parents and I ask that too. When we lived in our village near Prague, he was a nice person. He had friends, he did well at school. But he hated moving here. He didn't make friends. He got bent out of shape. We were so glad Sylvie liked him."

Matthew remembered that moment on Rachel's doorstep: how the person who answered the door had looked like her, dressed like her, yet been completely different.

Thirty-one

ZOE

"GIVE ME A minute, Ms. Lang," said the porter. "I think he left a message for you." In the background she heard a girl's voice, her inaudible words punctuated by the merry ring of a bicycle bell. Then the porter was back. "Can you meet at the bookshop at four p.m.," he read, "Wednesday, or Thursday?" After a hasty calculation—school, excuses, buses, enlisting Moira—she said Thursday but not until five.

As soon as she stepped into the brightly lit shop and caught sight of him, standing beside a table of books, she knew something had shifted; he was pleased to see her, but not entirely. "David Hume is one of my heroes," he said, holding up a history of the Scottish Enlightenment. "Shall we get some coffee?"

"Can we go to your room? I don't have to meet Moira until ten." She held on to his hands, swinging them gently, and widened her eyes, both flirting and playing at flirting.

He made excuses—he wanted to talk; he hadn't tidied up—and when she said, "Please. We can talk there," yielded. In the street he seemed to forget his doubts. As they passed a shop already garlanded for Christmas, he told her about the Amish communities near Cedar Rapids, some of which celebrated Old Christmas on January sixth.

"They're very devout," he said. "Most of them won't have anything to do with technology."

"That must be hard," Zoe said. She was still trying to decipher his hesitation.

In his room the vase on the windowsill held red tulips. Again, she wondered who had bought them, but he was unzipping her jacket and his own, and they were in bed, having another kind of conversation, first tumultuous, then peaceful.

"Zoe, Zoe, Zoe."

He reached for the bedside light; the small room glowed around them. "Zoe," he said, sitting up in the narrow bed, "I've fallen head over heels in love with you."

Did she speak? Later she couldn't remember because he was still talking, and he was saying that he should have told her. He had a girlfriend; she was living in Paris this term. He was going on Sunday to visit her. So when he had claimed, weeks ago at the café, that he wasn't looking for a relationship, it was because he already had one.

"For how long?" she said.

"Ten days. I'm sorry. At first, we weren't going to do anything, and so there was no need to tell you. I meant to, that day we went for a walk—I should have; I knew where we were heading—but I was afraid I'd never see you again. There's no excuse. I was a coward. I swore I wasn't going to go to bed with you again without telling you. When I saw you in the bookstore, I couldn't stop myself."

Then she asked all kinds of questions. How long had he been with Renée? Was she American? Did she have other boyfriends? What did she do? He'd been seeing her for the last year. She'd never mentioned having other boyfriends, but he'd never asked. She was married to a rather eminent physicist and was doing research at the Sorbonne into Simone Weil. She lived in Chicago and had started an organization to provide tutoring in inner-city schools.

"Will you tell her about me?"

"Yes. She has to lie to her husband—right from the start she made it clear he would always come first—but we've always agreed there's no point in having an affair if you can't be honest."

"So she won't mind?"

Once again she sensed his hesitation. "In theory," he said, "she believes that jealousy is a symptom of the male patriarchy, the long history of men owning women, and women's resulting insecurity. In practice, she's a very passionate person." He looked down at her, lying beside him. "Don't you want to yell at me, tell me I'm a son of a bitch for deceiving you, say you'll never see me again and storm out?"

"I don't know," she said.

She remembered her mother's mysterious suggestion that feelings were optional. Now emotions were leaping up, swirling around, volunteering, vanishing, some dimly recognizable, some barely apprehended. Any number of postures seemed possible;

none, so far, insisted. She knew she didn't want to shout. She knew she was already, even as she lay beside him, missing him. Was she jealous? Angry? Sad? Stunned? Bewildered? Outraged? She couldn't tell. She felt reluctant to single out one from among the throng; whichever she chose, perhaps seized almost at random, would begin not just to describe but to dictate her response. She pictured him in Paris, gazing up at the doorway of Notre-Dame and its carvings of the Last Judgment, walking by the Seine, wandering through the Latin Quarter, sitting in the Place des Vosges. She pictured him holding hands with a tall woman with long, tangled brown hair and a wide smile.

Thirty-two

DUNCAN

WAS IT BEING the only one without a job that made him feel becalmed? Matthew was working extra shifts at the Co-op; Zoe was working Saturdays at the butcher's; his mother wore her busyness like a tightly buttoned coat; his father claimed projects and deadlines. Day after day he waited for his parents to suggest what he, or they, must do to try to find his first mother. On Saturday morning, after Matthew and Zoe left, he cleared the kitchen table and spread out a dozen sheets of colored paper. At supper the night before they had studied his sketches for the family Christmas card and chosen the partridge in the pear tree perched on a sleigh, drawn by two geese. He was outlining the tree when his mother came in; she had to make a carrot cake for her ancient Greek party. As he drew the branches, she peeled the carrots, the muddy skin slithering off to reveal the bright orange. A tricky color to use in a painting; maybe if one chose other colors from that end of the spectrum—glowing pinks, searing reds—it could work.

"I phoned directory inquiries for London," she said. "All the different areas. There's no listing for your mother, but I made a note of everyone with the same surname. I thought I could call and ask if they knew her."

"Can I call?"

The peeler paused. "I worry people may think we want to find her for a bad reason, to hurt her, or get something from her."

It was her job, he knew, to think of the worst thing that could happen, and guard against it. "But we don't want to hurt her," he said. "We just want to talk to her."

"You sound like a teenager."

She began to grate the carrots. What was she trying to tell him? Could he ask? Or would that detonate another of those little bombs he'd been setting off recently? He drew a pear, then a second smaller pear.

"People will wonder," she went on, "why a boy your age wants to speak to a woman her age. We might inadvertently hurt her. Hurt her," she explained unnecessarily, "without meaning to."

Oh, he thought, she's trying to say I'm a secret. "You phone," he said, "and I'll listen."

"Quietly," she insisted.

"Very quietly. Can we call now?"

"Give me fifteen minutes to get the cake in the oven."

He picked up the drawing of a goose and began to cut it out, trying to make each bite of the scissors flow into the next. In twenty minutes he might know where his first mother lived.

He carried the hall phone up to the study and, keeping a careful distance from the cactus with its stingers, stationed himself beneath the windowsill. His mother headed for her desk. Then she stopped and came to kneel beside him. "You're very brave," she said.

"Not really." The little mermaid had cut off her tongue to reach the prince, danced on swords.

At her desk his mother opened a notebook. "Here we go." Slowly and deliberately she pressed the buttons on the phone; he heard the sound of ringing; after six rings a message began to play. Not a single syllable uttered by the growly man's voice was familiar. "He must be speaking Turkish," his mother said, and made a note in her notebook. She dialed the next number. It rang ten times; neither a human nor a machine answered. Again she made a note. The third time she dialed, someone picked up the phone.

"Hello," said a woman, her voice surprised, hopeful.

Everything stopped. He pressed his palm even more tightly against the mouthpiece.

"I'm sorry to bother you. I'm trying to contact Esmeray Yildirim. Do you know her, or know how to reach her?"

"Who is this?"

"My name is Betsy Lang. I'm a solicitor. I'm trying to find Ms. Yildirim for one of my clients."

"So why does he want to find her?"

His mother gave him a warning glance. "He has some information for her. Good news."

"You have the wrong Esmeray," said the woman. "Our aunt is still living in her village near Izmir. She's nearly eighty-four and almost blind. No one has good news for her."

"You're right. I'm not trying to reach your aunt. Do you know another Esmeray Yildirim, living in London, or nearby, aged around thirty?"

"I don't." The phone went dead.

"Goodness." His mother pressed her hands to her face. "This is harder than I thought."

"How many names do you have?"

"Seventeen."

"Let's do one more and take a break."

The next number yielded a man. No, no. He did not know of an Esmeray Yildirim. Had never heard of her. Sorry, sorry.

THE STENCIL OF THE FIRST goose was sleek and handsome, a little arrogant. The second goose, he determined, would be plumper, nicer. He was drawing the neck, trying to capture that goose-like straightness, when a ringing broke the silence. His palms, instantly, were slick with sweat. How had his body done that so quickly? And why, when it was just the phone ringing? His mother had gone off to her party. She had not left a number during any of her calls; there was no way Esmeray could know he was trying to find her. Yet even as he reached for the receiver, he imagined a woman with a faint Turkish accent, saying, "Am I speaking to Duncan Lang?" This was the season of miraculous encounters: people guided by stars, angels, coincidences.

"Hello," he said hesitantly.

A woman's voice, equally hesitant, no Turkish accent, returned his greeting. "I'm trying to reach Hal Lang."

"He's at the forge. He usually gets home around five."

"Are you Duncan?"

He admitted that he was. Before he could ask if she wanted to leave a message, she said goodbye. He tried to go back to working on the goose, but the phone call had left him restless. For the first time he thought about his search from his first mother's point of view. She had her life, good or less good, in which he played no part, and here he was, after nearly fourteen years, trying to walk into it: your son! Perhaps the room he had visited in his dream, the room he thought they shared, was hers. He was an intruder, trying to force the door. Perhaps hearing from him was the last thing she wanted. He might, as his mother had suggested, hurt her. He retrieved Lily's lead.

Outside dampness rose from the pavement, fell from the sky. Before they reached the end of the street, Lily's ears were pearled with droplets. At the crossroads she suggested the park but gracefully accepted his decision to go to the forge. He didn't need to talk to his father, only to make sure he was there. Passing the Co-op, he saw a familiar figure, arranging cans of soup. Matthew didn't notice his wave. Soon he and Lily were turning into the street that led to the forge. The large double doors were shut, as usual in colder weather. They walked round to the side door. As he read the modest notice one more time—*Blackberry Forge. Prop. Hal Lang. Hours: 7:30-4:30, or by appt*—he heard his father say, "It's not like that," and then a woman's voice. At once he was certain it was the woman he had just spoken to; she had come rather than phoning. He turned the knob, and the door, like every door for which his father was responsible, swung open, silent on its well-oiled hinges. With Lily at his heels, he stepped inside.

On the far side of the room, thirty or forty feet away, his

father and the woman were standing by the workbench, facing each other across several yards. She was very still, her hands thrust deep into the pockets of her jacket. Such stillness, he knew from the afternoon he'd waited for Karel, took resolve. His father had his arms outstretched, as if he were trying to reach her but did not dare take a step closer.

"I thought you were happy with what we had," he said.

"I thought so too, but something changed after that weekend in Wales. I started to have fantasies of whole days together, whole nights, of not having to hide, or make excuses, or feel like a bad person. Then, when I had the accident"—she stared off in the direction of the anvil—"I couldn't call you."

"Your brother came to the hospital. You're better now."

"Exactly. I'm thirty-five, and my next of kin is my brother, who has his own lovely partner and two children."

His father let his arms fall by his sides.

"The baby is due on July third," she went on, "but my doctor says first babies are often late."

Why was she talking about a baby? She stood there, looking at his father, waiting. Her sentence seemed to reach him very slowly, then all at once.

"Oh, my god." He stepped toward her, stopped. "How could that happen?"

"The usual way."

In the street outside a horn hooted, tentative and plaintive. "How long have you known?"

"I've suspected for a while. Known for a week." Her forced calmness was slipping.

"So at the pub, when you said you had a headache and wouldn't have a glass of wine . . ." He trailed off. "What are you going to do?"

"Take my vitamins, do yoga, avoid alcohol, hope that other people congratulate me."

"You mean you're going to have it?"

She moved her head fractionally. She's waiting, Duncan thought; she's giving him one more chance. His father backed away and sat down on the stool he used when he was working at the bench. He picked up a small hammer and hefted it from hand to hand.

"I know what you want me to say." He spoke as if he were being slowly crushed in one of his own vises. "But I can't. There have been times I thought I could, that I could have a new life with you. I know you sensed that, and I know it was misleading. We both began to talk differently, to forget what I said the first time we had a drink: that I could never leave my family. That was true then, and whatever I feel for you"—his voice faded, rallied—"it's still true."

"So when we talked about going to see Monet's garden, and walking the Pennine Way, and learning to scuba-dive, you were lying."

Her accusation flew through the shadowy space.

"In a way. Yes. I thought of doing those things with you. I truly wanted to. But I knew the chances of us actually doing them were very, very small. It was so much nicer to pretend we had a future."

"And, like it or not, we do. Touch wood"—she reached for

the workbench—"we'll always be connected, even if we never see each other again."

His father hit the bench with the hammer, a dull thud, once, twice. "I'm sorry," he said. "I don't know what to say."

"On the contrary, you know exactly what to say. You're saying the baby doesn't change things. You're saying you wish I'd get rid of her or him. You're saying you don't want to have another child, that you won't be a father except for DNA."

She spoke evenly, but Duncan could tell that each sentence was filled with pain. Stop hurting her, he wanted to shout. At the same time he dimly grasped that if his father did not hurt this woman, something terrible would happen to his mother, to Matthew and Zoe, to him. His father had begun, once again, to apologize when Lily, who had been standing quietly beside him since they came through the door, stepped forward.

The woman caught sight first of her, then of him. "Hello," she said.

He gave in and followed. "Hello. I'm Duncan. This is Lily."

As they approached, the woman bent down; Lily went to her and offered a paw. The woman shook it. Still kneeling, she looked up at Duncan. "I hear you're a fabulous painter. Do you have favorite artists?"

"I like this Italian painter who paints five bottles over and over."

"Morandi. He's sublime. When you're older, you'll have to visit the museum in Bologna."

"Have you been?"

"No." The woman's hair rippled pleasingly as she stroked

Lily. "But I'd like to. You can see the studio he had in the house he shared with his sisters."

"I paint in my bedroom. Do you paint?"

"Not really. I'm a graphic designer. I met your father when some friends asked me to help them design a coffee table."

While they talked, his father had risen to his feet. He was watching their exchange as if they were tossing a burning torch back and forth; any moment one of them would drop it.

"Dad, I wanted to ask if I could go over to Will's. I've got the Christmas card under control."

His father made a noise, neither yes nor no.

"I'd better be going," said the woman. "Nice to meet you at last." Before either Duncan or his father could say goodbye, she was gone, leaving the two of them alone.

When Will's little sister was born, Duncan had spent hours lying beside her on the rug, watching her eyes focus on a butterfly mobile or a stuffed animal. "You watch her like she's a TV," Will had said. Duncan had not corrected him, but TV was only sometimes interesting. Bethany was like the sky, interesting even when she was boring.

He took a step toward his father and found his path blocked by Lily. She was emanating one word: No.

No to what?

No to staying another minute, saying another word.

"Dad? I'm going to take Lily for a walk and go to Will's."

Pulling up the hood of his jacket, he followed Lily through the rainy streets to the park. What had just happened? A woman telephoned the house and then went to the forge, where she told his father she didn't want her brother to be her next of kin and that she was going to have a baby. She wanted his father to be happy about the baby. His father wasn't.

In the park Lily kept close. Because of the rain, there were no other dogs. He picked up a stick and threw it. She dutifully retrieved it and set it at the foot of a chestnut tree. Not today. He knew that married people had what were called affairs, that they were unfaithful, but those words didn't seem to fit. The woman was nice, he and Lily could both see that, and somehow his father had ended up hurting her, and hurting himself.

He walked across the sodden grass and took refuge beneath his favorite cypress. The thickly needled branches formed a canopy above him. A seagull landed nearby and began to peck at an abandoned bag of crisps. Watching it stab the bag over and over, he thought, The woman is like my first mother. Some man started me growing inside her and then wanted no part of us. Or perhaps she wanted no part of the man. The gull stabbed the crisps bag one more time and, stiff-legged, strode away. On or around July third he would have a brother or sister, and some day perhaps that brother or sister would be standing under a wet tree on a wet afternoon, wondering desperately about his or her father. At last he understood the lesson of the little mermaid. You could want and want and want and still be empty-handed.

Thirty-three

MATTHEW

FIVE IN THE afternoon, already dark. He was at the middle till, handing a girl a one-pound coin and two twenty-pence pieces, her change for a carton of orange juice and a loaf of bread, when a loud bang brought him, and everyone else, to a standstill. The air was filled with the sharp sounds of broken glass, the long ghastly scrape of metal on tarmac, a cry, another bang. A car had hit something—a lamppost? Another car? Matthew dropped the girl's change, closed the cash drawer, and ran out into the street.

The remains of the scooter were lying against the curb a hundred yards from the shop. Running toward it, searching for the rider, he saw only the wrecked machine, the back tire, severed, a few yards from the rest. It was as if the rider had vanished, catapulted into some other street, some other town, by the force of the collision. Then he spotted him lying, facedown, close to the gutter. People were already bending over him. Matthew recognized a familiar silver helmet.

As he knelt, a woman standing at Ant's feet kept saying "Don't touch him. Don't touch him."

From the helmet came a faint sound.

"Ant? It's Matthew. Can you hear me? Are you okay?"

Behind him, he heard the manager of the Co-op saying that an ambulance was on the way; he had called the police. Matthew repeated this to Ant. "You're going to be all right," he said. What did he know? But he tried to make his voice strong and confident. Cautiously he rested his hand on Ant's gloved hand. Around him people were asking, Had anyone seen the car? The woman who had been saying "Don't touch him" asked Matthew if he knew the driver of the scooter.

"Anthony Martin. He lives on Mulberry Lane."

She hurried away; he kept his hand on Ant's. If Zoe hadn't broken up with him, she might have been lying here too. He remembered, from books and films, that it was important to talk to an injured person, to keep them conscious. Once a person left consciousness, it was hard for them to find their way back. "I was on the till at the Co-op," he said, "when I heard the car hit you. The manager's been giving me extra hours since we finished exams. Zoe's got a job at the butcher's. Weird for a vegetarian, but she likes it."

Ant said something. Bending lower, Matthew heard "Help," and "Up."

"I can't, Ant. We have to wait for the ambulance. If you move, you might make things worse. Did you see the car?"

Above their heads, the woman said, "Your mother is on her way. She'll be here soon."

"Yes," whispered Ant.

"Yes, you saw the car?"

No answer. Before he could ask again, he heard sirens far away and then much closer. Just as with Karel, there were men and a stretcher and a lighted ambulance, filled with hopeful machines. He let go of Ant's hand, and at once Ant was surrounded. As the paramedics bent over him, he cried out. The hairs on Matthew's arms rose. For a moment no one spoke. Then one of the men said, "Let's get him on the stretcher while he's out."

As they carried him to the ambulance, Matthew saw the helmet, sitting alone on the pavement like some small, forgotten UFO. He was carrying it back to the shop when a spotlight lit up the street. "This is the police," a loudspeaker announced. "Can everyone stay where they are for a few minutes? We want to get names of witnesses."

Turning away from the beam, he spotted Tomas on the other side of the street. Before he could pretend not to have seen him, Tomas waved. He waved back, a small, breezy gesture. A couple of police officers, a man and a woman with clipboards, were making their way from person to person, noting names and phone numbers. People began to relax, setting down bags, asking each other what they'd seen, talking about the slippery roads and how people drove too fast. Matthew gave his name and number to the policewoman and explained that he'd been working at the Co-op when he heard the crash. He'd run out and seen the scooter lying in the street and knew it belonged to his friend. No, he hadn't seen the car.

She took this down, thanked him, and suddenly broke off. "Aren't you the boy who found the young man in the field?"

He recognized the policewoman who had accompanied Hugh

Price on his first visit. He admitted that he was. "Nice to see you again." She raised her swooping eyebrows. "I hope your friend's okay."

As soon as she moved on, Tomas was beside him, standing much too close, breathing hard. Beneath his watchman's cap, his eyes glittered. Surreptitiously Matthew took a step back. Did Tomas know he had spoken to Karel?

But Tomas was whispering, "I saw him. I saw the car."

"What car?" Despite himself, he too was whispering.

"The car that hit the scooter. It was baby blue. There was a dent in the rear bumper."

Around them people were scattering, heading for cars, shops, homes, as the police released them. "You mean it was the same car?" He felt a rush of vindication: their searching had not been pointless. "Did you tell the police?"

"I did, but they didn't understand."

"We should call the detective. I have his number."

"He made me feel guilty," Tomas said sullenly.

"That's because you didn't tell him you were playing with trains the morning Karel was attacked. Come on."

Inside the Co-op the manager was working Matthew's till, ringing up groceries with surprising efficiency. When Matthew asked if they could use the phone—it was an emergency—he held out the office key. "Be sure to lock up when you finish," he said. In the office Matthew retrieved Hugh Price's card and dialed the number. Beneath the bright lights, Tomas's excitement was even more apparent, his cheeks flushed, his breathing audible. A man answered the phone, and Matthew asked for Hugh Price.

He handed Tomas the phone and stepped away to the large window overlooking the shop. From this vantage point all four aisles were visible; only the meat and cheese counters, directly beneath, were hidden. Tomas repeated his story. In the pauses, Matthew guessed the detective's questions. The car had been going fast, yes, faster than thirty. No, the brake lights hadn't come on when it hit the scooter. In aisle two Matthew saw their neighbor, Mrs. Lacey, pick up a box of cereal, study the list of ingredients, and set it back on the shelf. She moved on to the pasta.

"He's coming to take my statement," Tomas said when he hung up. "Maybe they'll finally catch the bastard, and Sylvie will talk to me again."

Mrs. Lacey, now in aisle three, lifted a small jar off the shelf and, without looking at it, slipped it into her jacket pocket. "I've got to get back to work," Matthew said. Keys in hand, he headed for the door, but Tomas, instead of following, settled himself in the manager's chair. Did he think he could sprawl there until the police came? No wonder Sylvie had left him.

"Come on," Matthew said. "I have to lock the door."

It was a relief to be back at the till, ringing up groceries, making small talk, even while the shock of what had happened kept happening, over and over. As he rang up a tin of baked beans, a six-pack of beer, he thought of Ant, one minute driving home, the next flying through the air. That the driver might be the man who had hurt Karel was confounding.

AT HOME HIS MOTHER AND Zoe were sitting on the sofa, watching television. Still holding the helmet, he stepped in front of the screen and told them about Ant's accident.

"Christ!" Zoe was on her feet. "Is he all right? We have to phone the hospital."

"They won't give information to non-family members," said his mother. "We can call and leave a message for his parents."

"But what if—"

It took him a few seconds to understand what Zoe was asking. His mother said no, even if things were very serious the hospital couldn't tell them, but from what Matthew said, it sounded like the prognosis was good. Ant was conscious; he could talk. "I'll ask his parents to phone as soon as they can," she said, and left the room.

"Zoe, I really think he'll be okay. He was wearing his helmet." He held it out, proof. She was sobbing too hard to hear. He had seen Zoe with Ant a few times: once leaning toward each other at the cinema; another time standing by his scooter, arguing. Bewildered by this storm of emotion, he patted her shoulder, uselessly. When his mother returned, he told them, talking over Zoe's trailing hiccups, the other part of the story: that Tomas had recognized the car.

"But he can't have seen it for more than a few seconds," said his mother, "and it was already dark."

In the shock of the moment, he had believed Tomas unquestioningly. Now he felt stupid for not considering that Tomas, like one of his mother's witnesses, had seen what he wanted to see, conjuring the blue car out of desperation. "He was very definite," he said doubtfully.

"You sound like you know him." Between hiccups, Zoe was eyeing him curiously.

"He was collecting for Oxfam." Trying to change the subject, he said he'd seen Mrs. Lacey shoplifting. Only a small jar of pesto, but still.

"Oh dear," said his mother. "I didn't realize she'd started again."

"You mean she's done this before?" The Laceys lived a few streets away and had always seemed like law-abiding people.

"For years, on and off. Mr. Lacey goes in and pays for the items. It's usually a sign that she's sliding toward depression. The shopkeepers here all understand, but there've been a couple of nasty scenes in Oxford."

"I've never heard that shoplifting was a symptom of depression," Zoe said.

Thinking about Ant and the scooter, he asked if Dad was back. Maybe he'd be able to weld the pieces back together. It turned out Hal had come home early, complaining of a sore throat, and was already in bed. None of them knew what to do next. Watching television, unless it was the news, seemed heartless. His mother retreated to her study. Zoe went to take a bath. He went to his room and tried to focus on homework. He was studying a map of the Austro-Hungarian Empire when he smelled onions frying. Downstairs his mother was at the stove, wearing an apron.

"Mum, what are you doing? It's nearly ten o'clock."

"Making mushroom soup. It's been a trying day."

While he washed the mushrooms, she described her phone calls to people with the same surname as Duncan's mother. "Each time I feel like I'm lifting this huge weight. The truth is, I don't want to find her. If she's an addict, or an awful person, I don't want her having anything to do with Duncan. What if she says, 'I'll kill myself if you don't come and live with me?'"

"Here." He handed her the mushrooms. "She's much more likely to say she wants nothing to do with him."

"Which would be upsetting too. I can't imagine any scenario that is going to make Duncan happy. She was sixteen when she had him, younger than you."

He passed on Hugh Price's suggestion of a private detective, and she said that was on her list. "I want Duncan to feel we've done our best. Would you like some wine? There's a bottle of red open."

He poured two glasses; they sat down at the table. Then she got up again to fetch some biscuits and cheese, and they were both eating ravenously. "Are you okay about Rachel?" she said, slicing into the cheddar.

"I miss her, but"—he hadn't dared say this aloud before—"I can tell I won't soon. What upsets me is that she wasn't the person I thought she was." The others were nearby, but it was as if he and his mother were alone in the house, talking as equals.

She raised her glass. "You're like me. You like clarity. That's why I wanted to study law." They each cut another slice of cheese. "I don't mean to put you on the spot," she went on, "but I'm worried about Zoe. Do you know what's going on with her?"

He had been braced to say he knew nothing, less than nothing, about his father's comings and goings. That Zoe was the subject of her concern brought him to an unrehearsed standstill. In the grip of his own double life—searching for Karel's assailant—it hadn't occurred to him that his sister might have one too. "I thought she was upset about Ant," he said.

His mother inclined her head; Zoe was fond of Ant, but not in that way. "She's been going to Oxford every chance she gets, and she agreed to babysit for the Dunns next Wednesday, even though Moira's having a party."

"Maybe she just wants to make some money."

"No, she's scheming, and the only reason I can think of why Zoe would scheme is a boyfriend. There must be something about this one that she knows will worry us."

"Like what?"

She ticked off reasons. "He's older, he's disreputable in some way, he's married, he's—"

"Married? Why would someone who's married want to go out with Zoe?"

His mother smiled. Suddenly they were no longer equals. "I don't want you to spy on your sister, but can you keep an eye on her? Let her know you're there if she's in trouble, though, please god"—she knocked the table—"not that kind of trouble."

Again, he was slow to catch her meaning, then amazed. Surely if Zoe were doing what he and Rachel had done, she would take precautions.

His mother poured the last of the wine into their glasses. "I hope a year from now we'll be sitting here and you'll have had a good first term at university and Duncan will be painting happily and Zoe will be working hard on her A-levels, and seeing a nice boy your age."

"And Dad," he improvised, "will have a second apprentice. And you—" He faltered. "What would you like, Mum?"

She faltered too. "Maybe your father and I could take a holiday? Go to Greece? I'll be able to read the inscriptions on the temples."

As she went to turn the heat off under the soup, he found himself talking about Karel. "We didn't tell you," he said, "but he said one word: 'coward.'"

"'Coward.' My sister used to call me that all the time, for not jumping into the pool or climbing a tree. As an adult, it's not a word you often hear."

"You're being a coward about phoning Duncan's possible relatives."

At once he was dismayed, but she was smiling ruefully. "You're right. I promised Duncan I'd do it, so I should get on with it. Well, time for bed."

Alone in his room, Matthew registered the chill—the heating had gone off for the night—and the pleasing fragrance of soup. His ears buzzed from the wine. As he brushed his teeth, he thought again about Zoe. She had been acting differently since she broke up with Ant, but he had attributed any changes to her worries about first their father, then Duncan. For half his life, he had been constantly in her company: going to the same school, playing in the park, turning the sofa into a fort. Now he realized how many hours there were each day when he had no idea what she was saying, or doing, or feeling.

Thirty-four

ZOE

PLEASE, SHE THOUGHT. She was sitting at the kitchen table, trying both to hear and not hear what her mother was saying on the phone to Ant's parents. *Please.* Then she was no longer sitting there, no longer thinking. She was hovering above the table, yet somehow still part of the living grain of the wood, the cool metal of the abandoned knife on the crumb-scattered plate, the smudge of butter on a napkin, the jar of marmalade, the note reading MILK, the ficus and the ferns.

Someone touched her shoulder; she was back.

"He's going to be all right," her mother said. Ant had cracked his pelvis and broken his right femur. They had operated for six hours. He had come round an hour ago and would love to have visitors in a few days.

"You're not crying, are you, Zoe?"

She was, though she scarcely knew why. "It was just so frightening: the idea he could be gone."

"It was frightening," her mother agreed. "Last night I kept thinking how glad I was you'd stopped seeing him. You could have been on the back of his scooter. If you hear Dad moving before you go, can you see if he needs anything? Be sure to remind him, I've rescheduled his customers. And could you pick up a pound of ham?"

On her way to work, she stopped at the newsagents to buy a get-well card for Anthony. The first customer of the day arrived as she was turning the sign on the door to Open. He asked for two pork chops and, if Mr. MacLeod could spare it, a bone for Shadow. Oh, thought Zoe. It hadn't occurred to her that she worked in Lily's favorite shop. That afternoon, along with her mother's ham, she brought home a nice greasy bone. She put the former in the fridge and set the latter on the floor, next to Lily's basket. Upstairs Duncan was sitting at his desk, Lily at his feet. She told him about the bone.

"Thanks," he said.

"Would you'd rather I didn't?"

"No, she likes being treated like a dog sometimes."

"But"—she wrinkled her forehead in imitation—"you're scowling."

"There's something I need to talk about. Can we go to the park?"

She checked whether her father needed anything—he didn't—and they put on jackets and scarves. As the three of them headed down the street, she described how many phone orders she'd taken; how she sounded like an expert when people asked what size of turkey they needed. Duncan listened and nodded. She knew he wouldn't want to talk until they were safely in the park, surrounded by twilight and trees. At the entrance, Lily spotted the Jack Russell she liked. The two began running in dizzying circles, the black dog following the mostly white dog following the black dog. Duncan led the way down the main path. Walking beside him, she felt the first hint of water seeping into her shoes.

As they passed the grove of birch trees, he said, "Something strange happened yesterday." A woman had phoned the house, asking for their father. She had known who Duncan was but hadn't given her name. And then, when he walked over to the forge, she was there—he recognized her voice—talking to their father. He had stayed by the door, and they hadn't seen him.

Zoe prickled with expectation. "Were they having a row?"

"Worse than that."

"Worse how?"

He shook his head in frustration. "She wasn't raising her voice, or saying horrible things, but she was really, really upset. When she went to the hospital after an accident, she had to name her brother as next of kin."

A fragment of some story they would never understand. "What did Dad say?"

"That she'd been okay in the hospital. He didn't get what she meant. But that wasn't the big thing." He walked around one puddle, splashed through another. Out of the gloom, Lily trotted toward them and began to walk a few yards ahead. "She said she was having a baby in July."

"A baby?" In all her worried imaginings about her father and the woman, she had never considered this possibility. They both stopped walking in the middle of the path.

"You sound as if that's terrible," Duncan said. "I like babies, at least the ones I've met."

The Jack Russell's owner appeared, walking briskly, and side-stepped them with a nod. Christ, if she'd overheard, Zoe thought, and started walking again. Duncan fell in beside her. "So that's why Dad's taken to his bed," she said.

"He was very upset, but he said it didn't change things. He couldn't do anything differently. He kept calling the baby 'it,' trying to make her or him go away. Then they saw me."

"He must have thought the world had ended." From a nearby tree a rook cawed; another answered.

"You know how in books they talk about someone going white as a sheet? He went completely pale. She talked to me about art—she's a graphic designer—and then she left." He glanced over at her. "I've been thinking this baby is related to us. Do you think that's true?"

"Yes," she said slowly, "but we must never, ever let Mum know. She might not be able to forgive Dad, and then everything would be unbelievably awful."

"Now there'll be two people I'm related to and never see."

He sounded so forlorn, she put her arm around him. "Oh, Duncan."

"I liked her. She wasn't angry when she saw me standing there. I could tell she was doing something hard, talking to Dad and not crying, or shouting. I think she'll be a nice mother. She won't give her baby away . . ."

Silently she finished his sentence: *like my mother.* For the first time she grasped that his life had begun with rejection. "This has to be a total secret," she said. "We shouldn't talk about it, even just the two of us, until we're grown-ups."

"The last, last thing I want is to make Mum more upset." He bent to pat Lily, and his voice was muffled. "I hate thinking I'll have a sister, or brother, I never see."

"Me too." Staring at the lights of the town, some orange, some white, some twinkling, it came to her that even as she and Duncan walked and talked, somewhere, not far away, cells were steadily multiplying. Next summer there would be a new person in the world, a person with whom they shared nothing, and half of everything.

As they walked back to the entrance of the park, a more immediate worry loomed. Their mother would take one look at them and guess that something was wrong. "Let's ask if we can have supper in front of the TV," she said.

"Good idea. Mum will think you're fretting about Ant and I'm fretting about my first mother. You're the one who's more likely to tell," he added as he unlatched the gate.

"Why do you say that?" She followed him and Lily through the gate and turned to latch it.

"Because you have boyfriends. Matthew told me one of the things you do when you want to let a girl know you like her is tell her something you've never told anyone."

What made her stop and stare back into the shadowy park was not the memory of herself and Rufus, lying in bed, exchanging secrets, but the realization that their conversation, which she had thought so utterly particular to them, was just what lovers did, what Rufus must have done with other girls, with Renée. How often had he told the story about the bear clock? Among the dark trees nothing moved. This feeling—quick as a mousetrap, sharp as a thorn—must be jealousy.

Thirty-five

DUNCAN

THROUGH THE WINDOW of the bus he watched the sun, glowing palely above the leafless branches of the elms and beeches. He was wondering how he would paint the sharp winter light, when the bus rounded a bend. A bright parenthetical shape appeared beside the sun. Something's happened, he thought. He kept his eyes fixed on the sun dog until the first houses hid it from view. Hardly able to contain himself, he walked to the front of the bus. When it stopped, he jumped down the steps and ran all the way home. Not pausing to take off his jacket or drop his bag, he followed Lily up the stairs. His mother was standing beside her desk.

"Did you find her?" he said.

Her lips formed a word beginning with a letter like a person with outstretched arms, ending with a letter curled like a snake. YES. YES.

His mother reached out her hand, and he took it. Then they were both sitting on the floor with Lily beside them. "It was the second-to-last phone number," she said. "I didn't want to dial it because I didn't want to get to the end of the list. As soon as you left this morning, I forced myself to call. The first time I got a busy signal. Twenty minutes later a young man answered. I said my little speech about trying to find Esmeray. The young man said, 'You mean my sister. Let me see if she's here.'

"When a woman said, 'Hello. This is Esmeray Yildirim,' I forgot all the things I'd rehearsed. I said 'My name is Betsy Lang, and thirteen years ago my husband and I adopted a three-day-old baby boy.' When she said 'Is he all right?' I knew I was talking to your birth mother."

"My first mother," he corrected, still trembling.

"Your first mother. I said you were fine; you'd been wondering about her. I told her we lived in Oxfordshire; that you'd like to talk to her. She said you could phone her today. Tomorrow she goes to Ankara for Christmas."

She had been waiting, she too had been waiting. "Where's her number?"

"Here." She handed him a piece of paper. "And I pinned a copy to your noticeboard."

Without even looking at the number, he was on his feet.

His mother stood up too. "Are you going to call her?"

"If that's okay." Even the delay of that brief sentence pained him.

"You don't want"—she hesitated—"to think about what you'll say?"

"I'll know what to say." Lily nudged his calf. "Don't worry, Mum. I just want to hear her voice. She's not going to say 'Come and live with me.' If she does, I'll tell her you're my parents, this is my home."

But there was still some obstacle. He stared at her, bewildered. Had she found his first mother only to not let him talk to her?

She was looking over his shoulder at the cacti. "I haven't had a chance to tell your father," she said quietly. "Maybe you could phone him first?"

As she left the room, closing the door to give him privacy, he felt a rush of protective love. She could never know, but it made sense that he would speak to his father, who was about to have a secret baby, before he spoke to his first mother, who had had a secret baby.

He heard hammering and then his father. "Hello. Blackberry Forge."

"Dad. Can you talk for a minute?"

"Duncan! Let me step outside."

Why did his voice sound so strange? As the hammering faded, he understood: his father was petrified.

Then his father was back. "I can hear you now."

"Mum's found my first mother."

"She found her? That's amazing. Amazing. I don't know what to say. I never thought . . . I'm happy for you, Duncan. Very happy. Once you started asking about her, I hated that we might not find her."

"I'm going to phone her. I wanted you to know."

"You must tell me all about it when I get home. Good luck. Good luck."

Duncan pictured his father waving, wishing him Godspeed on his long voyage. He put down the phone and reached to stroke Lily. She looked at him steadily, not quite smiling. He studied the phone number, written in his mother's clear handwriting: here was the doorway he had searched for, night after night. He began to press the buttons on the phone. The dial tone became the ringing tone. On the fourth ring a woman said "Hello?"

He was holding the phone so tightly his hand hurt. "This is Duncan Lang."

"Duncan Lang. What a good name. I am Esmeray Yildirim. Thank you for phoning me. You're very brave."

Hearing his first mother echo his mother, he was suddenly sure everything would be all right. "Not very," he said. "Something happened in September, and I started dreaming about you."

"A good dream, or a bad dream?" She spoke as if either was interesting and acceptable.

"A good one—you were in a beautiful room—then bad ones when I couldn't find the room."

"So you kept looking for me. The room I am in now is not beautiful, but it is comfortable."

"What do you see from the window?"

"It's a big window, almost from the floor to the ceiling. I can see the usual things—trees, roofs, pigeons. But right now I'm not looking out of the window. I'm sitting on my bed, talking to someone I haven't seen in thirteen years."

"I'm in Mum's study. The window looks out on our road. One person has walked by since I dialed your number."

"Your mother sounds nice."

"She is. She's a solicitor. And Dad is nice too. He's a blacksmith. I have an older brother, Matthew, he's in his last year of school, and a sister, Zoe, who's sixteen. And we have a dog, Lily." Lily raised her head.

"A good family. I share this house in North London with my brother and two friends. We all work."

"What is your work?"

"I'm an air hostess. I visit different cities and explore, which I like. I also serve food and drinks to many people, not all of them polite, which I like less."

"Do you paint, or draw?"

"No, but I make clothes. Sometimes people buy them. You must paint."

"I do. It's the one thing I'm good at." He asked which colors she liked, and she said there was a bluish green—sometimes statues turned that color—that she loved. And deep red. What about him?

He thought of the deep-red robe rippling beneath Leda and the swan. Perhaps they could visit the National Gallery together. "I like both those colors."

"In a few minutes I'm going to have to go. I still have some Christmas shopping to do. I don't know if your mother told you, but tomorrow I'm going to Ankara to see my parents, and the rest of my family. So how shall we end our first conversation?"

She did not say our family; they each had their own. The important thing was that she said "first conversation." Still he had to ask, "Can we talk again?"

"After I come back, in the New Year. We both need—"

She did not finish the sentence, but he understood. They

needed to think what they would be to each other. There was no name for their relationship; no road, already paved, to walk down. "Can I ask you three more questions?" Without waiting for an answer, he did. "What should I call you? Do you have other children? What is your address?"

"You should call me Esmeray. I don't have other children. I hope I will one day. I live at 39 Aberdeen Road, London N5. Thank you for phoning, Duncan. I hope you have good dreams tonight. Bye-bye."

"Bye-bye, Esmeray."

As the phone went dead, he realized he had forgotten to ask if she had given him a name. Next time. He wrote the address beneath her number, dropped the phone, slid to the floor, put his arm around Lily, and closed his eyes. After his long voyage, he had arrived. He had spoken to his first mother. She had said his name. He had said hers. She liked that blue-green color. She could see trees and chimney pots from her tall window. Then someone was stroking his back. And he remembered he had a mother who was right here. That she had listened when he asked for help, even though she didn't want to, even though she was afraid. He sat up and smiled at her.

"Mum, you're great."

Thirty-six

ZOE

HE DIDN'T WRITE. He didn't phone. Why should he? They
had said goodbye without promises or ultimatums. If he wanted
her, he would come back. What else meant anything? He was
wandering through the Louvre. He was climbing up to Sacré-
Coeur. He was sitting in the café where Sartre and de Beauvoir
had met, and always there was a woman beside him, a woman
who knew more than Zoe, who led a larger life, who could claim
both a husband and a lover. Yet everything that had happened
between them was still there: vivid, undeniable. When they
were walking by the river, he had described a new kind of logic,
fuzzy logic, in which there were more than two choices. The
world wasn't divided into X and not X. There was maybe X and
almost X and almost not X. At the library she had come across
a quotation from Spinoza: "Fear cannot be without hope nor hope
without fear." Perhaps that was an example of fuzzy logic. Since
Ant's accident, her daydreams were haunted. She imagined Rufus
carelessly crossing the street, hit by a car, or leaving a cathedral,

struck by a falling gargoyle. No one would tell her. No one would know she had mattered.

At Holywell Manor she dropped off an envelope; inside no note but a leaflet for the Salon of Second Chances. Then she bought some sausage rolls at the Covered Market and caught the bus to the hospital. Anthony's mother had given her directions to the orthopedic ward. As soon as she stepped inside, the bright lights and busyness made her feel better. "Room thirty-one," the nurse said when she asked for Ant. Two corridors later she paused in the doorway of a drab room. One bed was empty. On the second, the sheets were raised into a tent beyond which were the head and shoulders of a person, a boy person, lying against several pillows.

"Ant?"

"Zoe. Thanks for coming."

With his voice came the slow tide of recognition. Only his hair, she thought as she approached the bed, looked the same. Dark shadows circled his eyes, and his jaw was swollen a savage purple, fading at the edges to greenish yellow. She pulled the single chair close and laid the bag of sausage rolls on the bed. "How are you?"

"Bored out of my mind. It was okay being here when I felt lousy, but now that I feel better, I can't stand it. The cast makes it hard to sleep, and they wake me at six in the morning. A physical therapist is coming tomorrow to show me how to use crutches. After that I can go home."

"Brilliant. You can come carol singing."

He grimaced. "Please don't. Everyone keeps telling me how

lucky I am. I was riding home from chess club. Why should I have to be glad I didn't die? That I'll need crutches for four months?"

She recalled Rufus saying that the consolations of philosophy were overrated. In the corridor a trolley trundled by. "You're lucky like someone who survived the blitz," she said. "Your house was bombed to smithereens but you still have your smelly brown cardigan."

"Exactly." With painful slowness he raised himself against the pillows. "You know, they caught the driver of the car."

"No!" She managed, barely, not to jump to her feet. If Tomas was right, then the man, the man who stabbed Karel, was under arrest. How could the universe have shifted so momentously and she not known?

Ant didn't seem to notice her agitation. A policeman had come by this morning, he explained; a garage had recognized the description of the car. "I tried to tell him it was partly my fault," he said. "There's a huge pothole by the bus stop. I always swerve around it."

She had a sudden memory of them riding home from school, slowing to go over the speed bumps outside the primary school, passing the church, and then, just before the Co-op, looping into the middle of the road. "But he should have stopped," she said. "That's what you do when you hit someone: stop and make sure they're okay. It's good they caught him."

"I suppose, but I'm still lying here. I won't be able to ride my scooter again until summer. How's the butcher's?"

The old Ant would have wanted justice, she thought. Or revenge. But of course, he didn't know about Karel. For a moment she was tempted to tell him about finding the boy, about the driver of the car luring him into the field. "Have a sausage roll," she said. "Everyone makes fun of me for working there, but Mr. MacLeod is nice, and Dad is tickled because his mum worked there thirty years ago."

He sent her to the bathroom for a paper towel. Using it as a napkin, he ate a sausage roll in three bites. Reassured by his greed, she asked if he had seen anything after he was hit. "A white light? Someone waiting to welcome you?"

"What are you talking about?" He reached for another roll.

She thought of telling him about Meresamun, the mummy, and the different parts of the soul, but that would only confuse him further. Instead she said, "Didn't you see that television program when people who'd almost died described what it was like? How they saw a white light at the end of a tunnel, and a person, some-times it was Jesus, sometimes it was a family member, waiting to welcome them."

"I don't believe in Jesus," he said between bites, "and I wasn't close to dying. I never knew you were superstitious."

"I'm not. Maybe no one wanted to make you welcome." Until a few months ago she had believed that there was a word for ev-erything. Now life seemed full of occasions that left her speech-less.

Ant held out the empty bag. "Delicious! Moira says you've met a tall, dark stranger?"

She reached for the hem of her sweater and pulled it over her head, hoping the warmth of the room would account for her flushed cheeks. "I wish. There was someone, but he was just passing through Oxford." She laid the sweater in her lap. "Do you know Gordon Enright?"

He didn't. She described Gordon and his visit, laying a trail of bread crumbs that led away from Rufus. "And then he finally got a part because somebody sprained an ankle," she was saying when Ant's mother arrived.

"What a wretched evening," Mrs. Martin exclaimed. "You're so lucky to be snug inside."

As Zoe watched, Ant, without even moving, receded into the pillows.

Thirty-seven

MATTHEW

SOMEHOW, HE HAD thought, once they caught the man, he would be able to talk to him. But that was absurd. He wasn't a policeman; he wasn't a priest, or a doctor, or a psychiatrist. Why would he even be allowed to meet him, let alone ask him about Karel? After Zoe came home and broke the news, he heard ninety seconds on the radio. *Police solve two cases in one. Hit-and-run driver turns out* . . . The short paragraph in the local newspaper was painfully bare of motivation. The driver was thirty-two, sold farm supplies, no previous record. Yet again, Matthew made his way, empty-handed, to Oxford and the police station.

"I'll see if he's available," said the policeman behind the counter. "Take a seat."

He chose the chair beneath the noticeboard with its few safety posters and began to count the linoleum floor tiles. Why did it matter what had happened that day in the field? Some maniac had stabbed a boy and left him to die. The papers were full of such crimes. But he had seen Karel lying there, his legs red with blood, the swallows stitching the air. He was beginning to think the detective had refused to see him when the policeman called his name. The interview room was identical to the last one— ocher paint, scuffed table, two chairs—and sharply colder than the room where he'd been waiting. He was standing beside one of the chairs when Hugh Price stepped through the door.

"How's your brother?" he said.

"We found his birth mother. She isn't any of the things we dreaded."

"That's excellent."

They sat down. Across the small table the detective watched him, unblinking, unsmiling. It was clear he was not going to speak again. No wonder, Matthew thought, people confessed. "I know you're busy," he said.

This was not even worth acknowledging.

He played his one card. "I got Tomas to phone you. I was hoping you'd tell me about the man who stabbed Karel and hit Ant."

"Why?"

There it was: the single, implacable syllable to which he himself had only the flimsiest of answers. "I don't really know. Since that afternoon in the field, everything's been different." He did not stop to enumerate: Duncan, Rachel, his father, Zoe, even Mrs. Lacey. "That's why I helped Tomas look for the car. I thought if we could find the man, if I knew why he did what he did, things would go back to normal. Or"—he was too old for fairy tales— "I'd understand why they were different."

Something changed in Hugh Price's gaze; he took in Matthew anew. "My diagnosis," he said, "is that you're wrestling with the problem of evil." He spoke with a certain satisfaction, as if offering a sandwich to a hungry man. "For what it's worth," he went on, "I'm twice your age, and I'm still wrestling with it. Nothing prepares one for the discovery that there are people who have no conscience."

Abruptly he fell silent. Matthew sat very still, trying not to interrupt whatever visions, or memories, the detective was confronting. A minute passed. Two.

"This is quite irregular," he said. Loosening his tie, he leaned forward and began. "The man was driving out of town, on his way to a meeting, when he saw a boy standing beside the road. He'd never picked up a hitchhiker before, but he was anxious about the meeting, and the boy, when he bent down at the window, had a kind smile. They started talking, and the man heard himself telling the boy things he'd never told anyone. 'I'm not bonkers,' he told me. 'I knew I couldn't ask a total stranger to stay and talk to me.' He decided to pretend the car was overheating. He pulled over, emptied the bottles he kept in the boot, and persuaded the boy to come and look for a water trough.

"But in the field things started to go wrong. When the boy said he was going to flag down a car, the man panicked and hit him with one of the bottles. Then he took the bottles back to the car, fetched a blanket and an apple. He had a set of knives on the backseat, a wedding present for his sister, and he brought one to peel the apple. He sat on the grass beside the boy and started talking."

So the apple peel was a clue, Matthew thought, and he had thrown it away.

"At first the boy listened like he had in the car, peacefully, almost smiling. Then, suddenly, he swore. The man isn't exactly sure what happened next, but there was all this blood."

Matthew remembered the flies circling and circling.

"He seized the blanket, ran back to the car, and shoved the boy's backpack into the ditch. It wasn't until he was in the meeting that it occurred to him that people died when they lost too much blood. He planned to phone the police as soon as possible. But the meeting was followed by lunch, and another meeting. Then it seemed too late. He decided to go back to the field. If the boy were still there, he'd take him to the hospital. He thought he'd missed the gate when he saw your brother, standing by the side of the road."

"He just wanted to talk to him? He stabbed him so he could talk to him?" He could feel himself sweating in the chilly room.

The detective nodded. "More or less."

"And what about with Anthony?"

"That was pure bad luck. He was following the scooter, probably a bit too closely, when it swerved. He was sure he'd killed the driver, and that it was entirely his fault."

"So none of it was planned," Matthew said slowly. "If Karel hadn't decided to hitch, if the man hadn't left early for his meeting, everything might have been fine."

"If any number of things. He told me he'd never done anything like this before, and I believe him. I've met some monsters, people who would go to any lengths to get what they want. This man isn't like that. He feels guilt and he feels remorse."

"He'll go to prison?"

Hugh Price was on his feet, reaching for the door. "My job is to figure out crimes. I don't necessarily believe in punishment. You'll appreciate the irony." He gave his triangular smile. "I'd recommend you stay away from Tomas. Did I answer your question?"

"Yes and no. I wish it wasn't all so random." Then, surprised at his own daring, he handed the detective a leaflet for the Salon. "You don't have to dress up, or anything."

Back in the waiting room, a policeman and a policewoman were standing by the noticeboard, holding the arms of a girl around Duncan's age. Matthew was still taking in her filthy pink anorak and mud-streaked jeans, when her eyes fastened on him. "What are you bloody well staring at?" she demanded, and stuck out her tongue.

Thirty-eight

ZOE

SHE WORKED EXTRA hours at the butcher's, she helped her mother buy groceries, she helped Duncan deliver Christmas cards, she helped her father and Matthew with preparations for the Salon, she brought Lily so many bones they filled the freezer. She watched her father; deep inside he was forging a fence, twisting the red-hot railings into place, between his feelings for them and his feelings for the woman. In the evening he opened a bottle of wine while he made dinner. Sometimes he was almost silent as they ate; sometimes he couldn't stop talking. She and her brothers listened attentively or talked animatedly, united in their efforts to make sure their mother noticed nothing. One night, when they were eating pasta with leeks and smoked salmon, he asked if he'd ever told them how his mother foiled a bank robbery.

"Definitely not," Zoe said. Her brothers chorused agreement.

"This is a good one." He refilled his glass. "I must have been eight or nine, and I'd gone with her to the bank. We were standing in the queue when a man came in with a scarf over his face, which was odd because it was a nice day, and carrying a fat walking stick, which was odd because he looked young. He raised the stick to his shoulder. Suddenly it was a rifle, and he was shouting at everyone to lie down. The other customers started to obey, but Mum said, 'Philip, is that you?' He was our neighbors' oldest boy. She walked over, took the gun, and made her deposit."

"Wasn't she worried he'd shoot her?" Matthew said.

"That's what Dad asked. She said no, Philip couldn't even dig a hole in a sandpit. He must have seen something on TV, and got this daft notion about robbing a bank. I wish you'd known her," he added, "before she got ill."

"At least we knew her," Duncan said. "I drew a picture of her before she died."

"Do you still have it?" said her father.

While Duncan went in search of the drawing—he kept his work in boxes, by years—Zoe said that Mr. MacLeod often reminisced about her grandmother. "He was only a teenager, but I think he had a crush on her."

"That would make sense," said her mother. "When I met her, Nora was the most beautiful woman I'd ever seen."

"Did she have boyfriends?" Even in despair, love was a subject of inexhaustible interest.

Her father nodded. "One night a couple of years after Dad died, she asked Joe and me what we thought of a farmer who lived near Witney. I'm ashamed to say we made stupid jokes and pretended not to know why she was asking." Across the table Zoe saw his hand clench around his glass. "She ought to have thrown us out of the house, and married him."

"Would anyone like seconds?" said her mother.

"Here." Duncan was back, holding out a slightly tattered piece of paper. "Remember, I was only four."

They clustered around. Looking at his wavering lines, Zoe remembered her grandmother's bed with its carved wooden headboard. She had insisted on bringing it when she moved in with them. Duncan had drawn the border of roses and leaves. And there, propped up on several pillows, her hair around her shoulders, was their grandmother, eyes closed, nose pinched, mouth open.

"May I have this?" said her father.

Duncan handed it to him. "I could make a better drawing now," he said, "but it wouldn't be the same."

FOR AS LONG AS ZOE could remember, they had all taken part in the town carol singing, but this year the singing was postponed, twice, because of rain. Finally, on the twenty-third, her father phoned the singers and planned the route. First, they would go round the streets—old people and invalids sent requests—and then they would station themselves outside the Co-op and collect money for charity. They were in the hall, putting on jackets and scarves, when her mother announced that she felt a cold coming on. "I'll stay here," she said, "and get supper." As Zoe passed out the carol books, she wondered if something more was amiss. Had her mother finally caught wind of her father's affair? Then they launched into "Good King Wenceslas," and standing in the frosty air, surrounded by the flickering lanterns, singing the words she had known all her life, she felt the present moment grow and grow until it was large enough, almost, to keep everything else at bay.

At the houses they visited, doors were flung wide; people stood on thresholds, listening appreciatively; elderly faces appeared at windows. At one house on Larch Street two women stood in the doorway, each holding a swaddled baby. "Thank you," they chorused when "Oh, Little Town of Bethlehem" ended. The taller one held out a twenty-pound note.

Zoe went over. "We're collecting for Save the Children and the Gatehouse in Oxford," she said. "How old are your babies?"

"Leo's ten days old," said the one offering the money.

"And Edith is five," said the other. "A Christmas baby." She turned the white bundle so that Zoe could see the cap of dark hair, the tiny nose.

She had forgotten how small new babies were, how perfect. She heard herself gasp, "She's adorable." As she hurried to catch up with the singers, she remembered the photograph of the woman standing on the beach, smiling. Why did you have to come and spoil our family? she thought. A sinkhole had opened beneath their sturdy house.

At home they sat around the dining-room table to count the money. Her father poured five glasses of wine. Duncan took a sip of his and went to fetch a ginger beer. He helped her count the coins, arranging them in little towers. They had raised two hundred and seventy pounds, almost fifty pounds more than last year.

"All due to my collecting," Zoe boasted.

After supper—jacket potatoes with various fillings—they scattered to their rooms to wrap presents. At the top of the stairs Lily hesitated before following Zoe. So I must be the one in most need, she thought. Beneath Lily's attentive gaze, she laid out presents on the bed, found wrapping paper, scissors, tape. She was wrapping the tubes of paint she'd bought for Duncan when there was a knock at the door.

"I wanted to check you're all right," said her mother.

"I'm fine."

Her mother stepped into the room and closed the door. "Forgive me, you don't seem fine. You keep gazing off into the distance, looking sad. I know you're worried about Ant but is there something else? Someone else?"

In her imagining of this conversation she had always denied everything but now that her mother was here, a few feet away, regarding her without a hint of judgment, she longed to confide the events of the last six weeks. "Something happened with a friend," she said. "Not someone you know. He's disappeared. I don't mean like a missing person; I mean from my life."

"I'm sorry. You and Matthew have had a bad autumn."

A giant NO streaked across Zoe's brain. Rachel was a stupid, spoiled girl. Rufus was her other self, her soul mate. But that was not how the so-called facts would strike her mother. She would see an older man who had taken advantage of Zoe, lied to her, abandoned her.

"If you want to talk," said her mother, "if I can help, let me know. I hope you feel better soon. Thank you for making an effort. It can't be easy—all this Christmas stuff—when you're feeling gloomy." She smiled in a way that suggested she understood gloom.

One day, Zoe thought, smiling back, I'll tell her—it will be a story with a beginning and an end. Then she thought, if Dad leaves her, I'll set fire to the forge. "Thanks," she said. "Are you feeling okay?"

She was thinking only of her mother's cold, but Lily jumped down from the window seat, trotted over, and stationed herself a few feet away, gazing up at her mother. Her mother gave one quick glance in Lily's direction. Then she looked back toward the window where—Zoe had not yet drawn the curtains—the dark night pressed against the glass. Watching the two of them, Zoe felt a huge, pulsing pressure. All at once she understood: her mother, too, had erected a barricade between before and after, speech and silence, and it was tumbling down, falling all around her. What if she stepped through the rubble to the other side?

Lily gave a short, sharp bark.

Her mother closed her eyes. She seemed, perhaps Zoe only imagined it, to sway slightly.

Then she opened her eyes. "Thanks for asking," she said. "I'm going to have an early night and count on you to be my sous chef tomorrow. Who knew my vegetarian daughter would become an expert at cooking turkey?"

She smiled, a different, too-wide smile, and left the room. As the door closed behind her, Zoe had one clear, undeniable thought: She knows.

Yes, said Lily.

But how?

Answers flooded in. Her mother could have seen her father and the woman in Oxford, or a friend could have seen them, or she had overheard him on the phone, or she had noticed his adventurous cooking, or he had talked in his sleep. She hadn't known at first, else she'd have gone with him to Wales in September, but somehow, since then, she had learned of his affair and kept both the fact, and her knowledge of it, from all of them. Now, surely, she must guess from her father's taking to his bed, his drinking, his moodiness, his mere presence, that it was over.

But it's not, Zoe reminded herself. Did she know about the baby? The question made her quake. She could not imagine what her mother, with her keen sense of justice, would do if she discovered the existence of their half sister, or brother. Even Lily, who was feigning sleep at the foot of the bed, didn't have the answer.

Thirty-nine

THE SALON OF
SECOND CHANCES

THE SALON OF Second Chances was held on the penultimate day of the twentieth century, from four to seven p.m. The normally somber town hall, with its sallow walls and fluorescent lights, was transformed by the garlands and evergreens left over from the primary school Christmas play, and by the colored lights that Anthony's mother had strung around the room. Matthew and Benjamin had each carried over their family Christmas tree, one spruce, one pine, and the two stood, brightly decorated sentinels, on either side of the stage. The long buffet table was lined with candles. At one end was an urn with a battalion of mugs. A saucepan of Hal's mulled wine simmered on a hot plate next to two trays of mince pies donated by the Co-op. Mr. MacLeod had brought fifty sausage rolls. There were cheeses and dips, Victoria sponges and treacle tarts. In the background a David Bowie CD was playing. The committee had asked for volunteers—all ages welcome—to come as the person or animal you would most like to be. Some people came as famous people, some as their younger selves, some as characters in books or films. A few people set up little scenes and waited to be visited but most wandered around, greeting friends and strangers. Everyone, disguised or undisguised, paid ten pounds; five for under-eighteens.

The manager of the Co-op, wearing a suit and a beret, carrying an unlit Gauloises, prowled the crowd as a member of the French Resistance. "I'd have been a wretched maquisard," he confessed to Zoe. "I can't kill a spider." Eileen, one of Matthew's fellow cashiers, came as a zebra. A girl from Duncan's class was a mermaid, with silver fish fastened in her hair and a scaly tail trailing behind her. His friend Will came as the polar bear in *His Dark Materials*, walking upright in a white bear suit, wearing a pair of spectacles. Mr. MacLeod was Capability Brown, the great eighteenth-century garden designer. With the help of his son, he had made a miniature garden in one corner of the hall. The barman at the Green Man came as a famous Irish giant, walking waveringly on the stilts hidden beneath his extra-long trousers. Several small children—Hansel, Gretel, Thumbelina, and Little Red Riding Hood—followed him. In their wake, the barman's wife, dressed as a wolf, preened her whiskers.

Duncan had known instantly who he wanted to be. He wore his only suit and had brought his easel and five bottles, which he set up on a small table. It would be a kind of blasphemy to try to paint them, but a sketch, using pastels, seemed possible. He had brought a book of Morandi's paintings—one of his Christmas presents—so that people could glimpse their evanescent beauty.

Matthew also wore a suit. Feeling faintly disloyal to Hugh

Price, he had come as Inspector Morse, carrying a bottle of Wychwood Hobgoblin and a copy of Ovid's *Amores*. He could not help envying Benjamin, who, as d'Artagnan, the fourth musketeer, wore a dashing wide-brimmed hat and high boots.

Hal had come as Christiaan Barnard, the doctor who had achieved the first heart transplant; he wore a white coat with a stethoscope dangling from his neck. In one hand he carried an artificial heart.

Zoe had not planned to dress up, but that morning she had asked to borrow the black robes her mother wore in court. Pinned to her chest was a red heart on which she had printed one of her favorite quotes from Spinoza: *Desire is the essence of everyone*. Like Matthew, she carried a book: a dictionary wrapped in brown paper, labeled *Ethics*. If he had gone to Paris for the ten days he'd intended, then he was back. If he was back, then he had got the leaflet about the Salon she had left at Holywell Manor. If he had got the leaflet, then . . .

Betsy had spent two days shut away in her study, making her costume. "You'll see," she said when any of them asked. Both Zoe and Duncan noticed the arrival of a woman wearing a long blond wig. The lower half of her black leotard was covered with brown feathers that tapered into black leggings. Her arms too were covered in feathers; outstretched, they became wings. Only when she stopped beside Duncan's easel did he and Zoe recognize their mother, the siren.

How perfect, Zoe thought. She saw her father, standing near the buffet, staring at the siren with an expression she could not decipher.

"Excuse me, Mr. Spinoza," said the giant, "can you tell me what to do about being so tall?"

"Enjoy the view?" she suggested. But he was already moving away on his stilts, calling apologies over his shoulder.

Now her father in his white coat was greeting a man and a woman both wearing ordinary clothes. The man had beautiful golden eyebrows. He could have come as a lion, Zoe thought, and the woman could have come as a lion tamer. She was imagining their costumes, a huge mane for him, a flared skirt for her, when she saw standing beside them, upright and unmistakable, the boy in the field. Her father was handing him the model heart, pointing to an artery. She made her way through the crowd.

"And may I present my daughter, Zoe," her father said. "Better known as Baruch Spinoza."

Mrs. Lustig came into focus, not as a lion tamer but as the woman who worked at the post office, selling stamps and giving out pensions. Frank Lustig said, "I'm glad to meet you. We learned about you in school. Which is more important: truth or beauty?"

"They're not in competition," she said firmly. "The important thing is to understand." According to her library book, Spinoza believed passionately in understanding.

Karel, still holding the heart, stepped forward. "You are the third person I must thank for saving me."

For a moment all she saw was his face and, cupped in one hand, the deep red heart. She fumbled for words, something about the field, the man. Whatever she said, his gaze grew instantly opaque, as if a second, secret eyelid had closed.

"That was the best Christmas present," his mother said, "knowing he was behind bars."

Her comment served to bring Karel back. Or most of the way back. Zoe watched his eyes follow a man in a stovepipe hat. I don't have to talk to him now, she told herself. He lives nearby. But there was something about the Salon, full of people in disguise, and indeed her own black robes, that licensed a certain freedom.

"Come and meet my brother, Duncan," she suggested. "He's a famous painter."

Karel handed the heart back to her father and followed. They passed a stout man dressed as a Jack Russell terrier and a boy wearing round glasses and carrying a goblet. "In the field," she tried again, "I was sure you'd gone down to the underworld, that you would bring back a message."

She stole a quick glance at Karel. He was studying the sign above the buffet: WELCOME TO THE SALON OF SECOND CHANCES. "All the stories I know about the underworld," he said, "are about people trying to get their wives or their daughters to come back. No one ever asks the wife or daughter if she'd like to stay. Maybe she would? But I never got there. I was lying in a field with rabbits, and flies, and bales of straw. I could see the birds flying over me. I could hear the three of you talking."

"So you weren't unconscious."

"I was in between. I knew where I was, and I went places inside my head where I felt safe: my bedroom, my father's workroom, my parents' village. I was walking along the river that runs through the village. On the other bank a family was picnicking—

grandparents, babies, children, everyone talking and laughing. If I could cross the river, I would be with them, surrounded by happiness. But the current was very strong. I could see the water rippling as if it had muscles."

Suddenly he was holding her arm, guiding her to another part of the hall. "There is a woman here I would prefer not to meet."

"Which one?"

"Red jacket."

Zoe spotted her: fair hair, broad smooth cheeks, the jacket much bolder than she was. "Who is she?"

"My brother's former fiancée."

"Let's go and look at Capability Brown's garden. Is your brother upset at being former?"

"Very. He blames me."

They skirted an astronaut, holding her helmet in one gloved hand.

"My boyfriend broke up with me." Even as she spoke, she scanned the room, hoping Rufus would arrive to contradict her. Karel gave the smallest nod.

"Do you remember," she went on, "when we were in the field, you said 'Cowrie'?"

"Your brother Matthew thinks I said 'Coward.' Your brother Duncan, 'Cowslip.'"

Coward? Cowslip? She gazed at his pale lips. The three of them had never talked about what Karel had said that day. It had been so clear; there had been no need. She remembered the detective asking if she was sure about "Cowrie." She had been. Now she wasn't.

Side by side, she and Karel surveyed Capability Brown's garden. Mr. MacLeod and his son had brought in a six-by-six frame and filled it with sandy soil covered with artificial grass. At one end rose a small hill with a bench on top, surrounded by birch trees. A silvery stream ran down the hill into a silvery lake. Beyond lay a formal garden and an avenue leading to an eighteenth-century manor house. Two peacocks were strolling down the avenue, followed by an elegantly dressed man and woman, all four heading toward the house.

"How is the boy on the scooter?" Karel said.

"All right, though he's cross about being on crutches for four months."

"So he isn't hurt in his mind?"

If only they could be sitting on the bench on top of the hill, gazing out across the garden. "No. He thinks he's partly to blame. He swerved to avoid a pothole."

"That's good. He'll get better more quickly if he isn't angry. I, too, am partly to blame. When the man opened his car door, I wanted to refuse, but I could see he was a person people often said no to."

On the other side of the garden, Capability Brown was tending his lawn with a little rake. His son placed a tiny blue bird in one of the oak trees.

"Sometimes," Karel said, "I think my English is at fault. I say 'no,' people hear 'yes.' I say 'sparrow,' people hear 'cat.' "

"Your English is fine," she said. But how was it that she and her brothers had each heard him so differently?

Across the garden, Mr. MacLeod looked up from his rake.

"You should dress like that for work. Do you like my garden? It's modeled on one of my most famous gardens at Harewood in Yorkshire, with a few details stolen from Blenheim."

"You must have a lovely view from the hill," said Karel.

"You do, and walking down the avenue. My gardens are meant to make you feel the power of reason. You can see your destination, and you can get there by various routes. People didn't travel much in those days, so they wanted a garden to have many vistas."

Before either Karel or Zoe could respond, a woman wearing a white lab coat—Marie Curie? Rosalind Franklin?—had accosted him. Still eyeing the peacocks, Zoe said, "Do you have a girlfriend? Or"—she felt rude for not considering this sooner—"a boyfriend?"

"Not at present. There was a person I thought I liked. I was mistaken." He paused as if looking down the avenue of that relationship. "Perhaps I want too much."

"Spinoza," she offered, "believed that our happiness is bound up with who we love. Did you have to identify the man?"

"Yes."

She saw he had spoken his last word on the subject. Across the room Matthew, in his elegant suit, was making his way toward them. Quickly she said, "There's something I need to ask you, but I can't figure out what it is."

"You can ask me any time. I only have one life. Thanks to you I'm here tonight."

She started to tell him about Rufus, the things that were still true: how at the café she had felt as if they'd climbed onto a small, high ledge; the story they'd each read, he in America, she in England, about the town where the happiness of many depends on the misery of a few; Meresamun, the mummy at the Ashmolean, with her blue eyes, her jackals . . . .

Once again Karel put his hand on her arm. "You must not lose a person so dear to you," he said, "if you can help it."

SINCE HE SAW KAREL ARRIVE, Matthew had been trying to reach him. As Inspector Morse, he thought, he could ask crucial questions. What was it like seeing your assailant again? Are you glad he's going to prison? Finally, he extricated himself from a girl dressed as an octopus and made his way to where Karel and Zoe stood beside the garden.

"Good evening," he said, offering Karel his hand. How had he and Zoe become acquainted?

"To whom do I have the pleasure of speaking?" said Karel.

"Inspector Morse, at your service. Perhaps you've seen me on television? Or read my books? You decided not to dress up."

Karel acknowledged the obvious. "I am grateful to have a second chance at being myself," he said. "But if I were dressing up," he went on thoughtfully, "I might come as a sheep, safe in my woolly fleece, surrounded by many other sheep. If anyone tried to steal me, or hurt me, I would hide in the flock and you would catch the thief."

Matthew made a serious face. "I'd sit at home, sipping scotch and listening to *The Marriage of Figaro*, and suddenly I'd remember the broken straw, lying in the doorway. It was the flautist from the traveling orchestra who'd tried to steal you. He wanted the straw as a mouthpiece for his flute, and his daughter wanted a pet sheep."

"We were on our way to visit Duncan," Zoe said, turning from the garden in a swirl of black.

She led the way past a middle-aged woman dressed as a schoolgirl. Nearby, sipping mulled wine, Matthew spotted an elegant Oscar Wilde in conversation with Mrs. Lacey. She wore a long gray dress with a sign: *Reader, I married him*.

Duncan was drawing his five bottles while Ant's parents stood watching. Zoe kissed them. Matthew nodded in what he hoped was a laconic, Morse-like fashion. Mrs. Martin reported that Ant had wanted to come but needed to rest. "He'd love to see you," she said.

Meanwhile Duncan had stepped away from the easel and was telling Karel that he had spoken to his first mother.

"I did not know you had a first mother," Karel said.

Duncan started to explain that he was adopted.

I'll talk to him later, Matthew thought. Now he should change the CD, compliment his mother's costume, and try his father's mulled wine. He was heading for the wine when he caught sight of another familiar figure. Hugh Price, wearing his usual jacket, smiling his triangular smile, was talking to the giant. Before Matthew could reach them, the two disappeared in the direction of the stage.

A minute later the detective reappeared, towering over the crowd. He had borrowed the giant's stilts and was taking small steps, calling out warnings as people scattered before him. He almost collided with the astronaut and for several seconds swayed wildly.

DUNCAN TOO WAS WATCHING THE detective. Once again Zoe was alone with Karel. Soon he would be gone. "You should talk to your brother's fiancée," she said. "Maybe if she gives up on you, she'll go back to your brother."

He looked over at the wolf, who was gnashing her teeth. "The truth is," he said, "I do not like my brother. It would be better for Sylvie if she met someone else. Someone kind."

"You shouldn't have to feel guilty about either of them." Her robes made it easier to offer advice.

He leaned forward and kissed her cheek. "You shouldn't have to be broken up with. We will tell each other what happens."

As he headed back to the garden, Zoe saw the woman in the red jacket make her way toward him. In another part of the hall, she glimpsed her father, in his white coat, offering something—she hoped it was the model heart—to her mother.

AWKWARDLY, WITH THE GIANT'S HELP, Hugh Price got down from the stilts. "That was great," he said. "Good evening, Inspector Morse."

"How did you know?"

"The Ovid. Should I be insulted you didn't choose to be me?" His lips twitched, signaling the joke.

"Why did you become a detective?" It was, Matthew realized, the question he had wanted to ask all along.

Hugh Price thrust his hands into his pockets. "Are you asking because you're dazzled by my accomplishments? Or you think my job is impossible?"

Neither, Mathew wanted to say, but before he could speak, a voice said "Matty."

Eileen, his fellow cashier, in her zebra suit, was standing beside them. He introduced her to the detective. "I haven't heard of you," she said. "Do you have a TV series?"

"Not yet. Would you excuse me while I have a word with Matthew?"

As she moved away, he turned back to Matthew. In a low, steady voice, he said, "On October twelfth, 1984, my sister Diana disappeared. We searched and searched. No one saw her after she left school, there were no clues; it was as if the earth had swallowed her. It turned out that it had. The following spring a farmer, ploughing his fields, found her. A week later the man who buried her was arrested. The person I most want to be is my younger self, skipping football practice that day to meet her at the school gates and walk her safely home."

Before Matthew could answer, he too had stepped away, slipping between those in costume and those in ordinary clothes, moving unobtrusively toward the door.

AT FIRST DUNCAN HAD BEEN standing at his easel, only pretending to paint—there were too many distractions; the lighting was bad—but gradually he became absorbed in the problem of how to model the largest bottle. He was applying short strokes of gray when he became aware of a man watching him.

He wore an old-fashioned dark suit and a floppy mauve cravat. One gloved hand held up a mask, the face of a pale, long-faced man with long brown hair.

"Why did you decide to make the neck fade away?"

His questioner, Duncan realized, was a woman. Reaching for a stick of purple, he quoted Mr. Griffin. "I want to abolish the tyranny of subject matter."

"We're meant to see not just a bottle?"

"Exactly. And to see it beside the others. That's important too."

"I like the way the purple makes the gray look." The woman tilted her mask. "Or do I mean the other way round?"

"Everything is relative," Duncan said, again quoting Mr. Griffin. "Who are you?"

"I'm Oscar Wilde, not long after I wrote *The Importance of Being Earnest*."

"I saw it on TV last year. You were funny. I'm Giorgio Morandi, an Italian painter."

"Thank you. I was very famous, first in a good way, then in a bad way."

"What would be a bad way?"

"Being charged with various crimes, being sent to prison. I probably shouldn't use the word 'famous.' More like infamous, or notorious."

"I was well known," said Duncan, "not famous. I lived with my sisters in the town where I grew up, but I wasn't a hermit. I traveled, and I had artist friends. I began to paint my bottles when I got older."

"So are you old enough to paint them?"

Duncan—he had been about to lay down a streak of gray—paused. "No," he said, "but I'm not really painting them; I'm imitating Morandi. Here's a picture by him."

Oscar Wilde stepped forward to look at the book lying open on the table. "I wish we could see the real painting," she said.

"Do I know you?"

The mask turned in his direction. "We spent nine months together and spoke on the phone a couple of weeks ago."

She lowered the mask.

Almost unthinkingly, he began to itemize similarities and differences. Eyebrows and upper lips, the same. Skin, hers was a little darker; eyelashes, hers were thicker. Eyes, he couldn't tell. Earlobes? Yes, they curved in the same way. Hair? They could have swapped hair, and no one would guess; his was a little longer. Hands? But she still wore her black gloves.

"Duncan."

"Esmeray." To say her name, in her presence, made him feel as if he could see every color on the spectrum. "Can I see your hands?"

She set the mask down beside the Morandi book and took off her gloves. He set his right hand on the small table. She did the same. For a moment he could not bear to look.

"We have the same hands," she said.

He saw his own brown-skinned, long-fingered hand, and next to it, almost the same size, the same brown skin, the same long fingers, the same curve of nails and half-moons, the same thumb not quite reaching the knuckle of the first finger.

"It seemed such a large thing for us to meet for the first time," she said. "I thought this might be easier. Or easier for me. I wasn't even sure I'd say hello. But when I saw you painting, I couldn't help myself."

"No, no," he said, not sure what he meant, but wanting to reassure her. "I sent you the leaflet. I wanted you to come. Would you like to meet my family?"

"Not today. They shouldn't have to meet me without warning. I'm going to leave now." She leaned forward and kissed him on each cheek. "Oscar Wilde isn't my alter ego," she said. "Not like you and Morandi. I only got back from Ankara yesterday and had to find a costume in a hurry."

"Who would you have come as, if you'd had more time?"

"Amelia Earhart," she said, and headed for the door.

ZOE HAD DELIBERATELY NOT WORN a watch, but as she wandered the hall, she kept catching sight of other people's. It was six thirty on the Co-op manager's; people were beginning to leave. He wasn't coming. Not X. It was as clear and simple as that. She would have to learn to behave as if they lived on different planets. She stationed herself by the mulled wine and filled a mug to the brim. She emptied it in a few swift swallows and refilled it. You must not lose a person so dear to you, Karel had said, but what could she do?

Her mother was standing beside her, holding out a brown feather. "These keep coming off. I should have sewn them on, rather than using glue."

Zoe took the feather and raised her mug again.

"This was even better than last year," her mother said, "like Halloween for grown-ups. I like being a siren for an evening."

"Did you lure anyone onto the rocks?"

"Not that I know of, except for Hal."

Looking at her mother's flowing blond hair, her scarlet lips, her feathery chest, Zoe thought, He hasn't told her yet. "Do you think," she said, "there are things a person can do that are unforgivable?"

"You mean noncriminal things? To be honest"—her mother plucked another feather—"I'm not sure I know what forgiveness is. You hold something in your mind without anger. Is that forgiveness?" The feather drifted to the floor. "You thought your missing person might come tonight. I'm sorry." She leaned forward to hug Zoe.

Suddenly there was a drum roll. Hal, in his white coat, was standing on the stage between the Christmas trees. "Thank you all"—he spread his arms wide—"for coming to the Salon of Second Chances, and making it such a success. The town will benefit from the funds we've raised tonight. We hope the New Year, the new century, brings everyone the second chance they want."

"Or need," someone shouted.

People started to clap. There were shouts of "Happy New Year."

He was wrong, Zoe thought. If not X was true, then X couldn't be true. There was no "maybe," no "almost."

Around her people began to separate into two groups: those

about to leave, those about to tidy up. She finished her wine and found a tray. She did not trust herself to carry it, but she could fill it with mugs and glasses. In the doorway, out of the corner of her eye, she caught a flurry of movement. Her heart gave one last hopeful leap. But it was only the giant abandoning his stilts and embracing the wolf.

Benjamin took the tray, and she started filling the next one. Someone turned up the music. Her father walked by, carrying a Christmas tree. On all sides the hall was being stripped of gaiety and possibility, returned to its institutional dullness. At home she would go directly to bed and trust the mulled wine to carry her away. Perhaps later she would wake to hear a sound she was now in a position to recognize: her parents making love. For a moment, standing there, a mug in one hand, a glass in the other, the longing that came over her was so fierce that she was ready to retrieve her coat, walk the fourteen miles to Oxford, and bang on the doors of Holywell Manor until the porter opened them and she could run up the narrow staircase to his room.

She felt the hall lift a few inches. Firmly she retrieved it. Here was a cup branded with lipstick that might be her mother's; here a glass with an inch of apple juice. She fetched a rubbish bag and emptied in leftover mince pies, slices of orange. Then she turned back to filling the tray.

"May I help you?"

The cup she was holding slipped through her fingers and bounced, unbroken, on the tray.

He was standing on the other side of the table, his El Greco eyes fixed on her. He looked like no one else in the room, no one else in the universe. He leaned forward to set the cup upright. If he were here only to explain why he couldn't see her again, she wouldn't listen. Explanations meant nothing. They were a rippling curtain of words that people hid behind.

"Zoe."

He came around the table and bent to read what was written on the heart pinned to her chest: *Desire is the essence of everyone.* "I should have guessed you were Spinoza," he said.

Slowly he straightened and held out his empty hands, not so much reaching for her as offering himself. "When I was with Renée, I just wanted to be with you. I told her, and I came back and sat in my room and waited to see if my feelings would change. They didn't. I thought perhaps if I told you at the Salon of Second Chances, you'd give me a second chance. But I got lost driving here. I was afraid you might have left."

He was wearing a navy-blue jacket with two sets of buttons, each bearing the imprint of an anchor; a red tartan scarf framed his beard.

"Did you tell Renée about the bear clock?"

"The bear clock? Oh, you mean the one at the carnival. No, I never talked about that with Renée. Or anyone else."

They were still standing beside the table when something made Zoe turn. Across the almost deserted hall Duncan, still in his suit, was walking toward them, led by Lily. When he dropped the lead, she continued, ignoring the groups of people and the many fragments of fallen food in her path.

Zoe found herself sinking to her knees, her black robe pooling around her. Beside her Rufus too knelt—he seemed to understand the solemnity of the occasion. He held out his hand. A few feet away Lily halted. Eyes bright, ears pricked, she regarded him thoughtfully, taking in his virtues and his faults, his desire for the straight roads of reason and his longing for the winds of passion. Zoe, she knew, believed this man was her Platonic ideal, her other half. They all three stayed quite still. Then Lily seemed to reach a decision.

Forty

THE DEGREE SHOW

HERE IS WHAT happened eight and a half years later, on a Thursday shortly before the summer solstice. The three Lang children were making their separate ways to the hall in central London where Duncan's degree show was being held. He was sharing the space with eight other students: six painters and two sculptors. When he took Lily for a walk that morning, he could feel the heat already gathering, along with his own anxiety. While she examined a rowan tree, he studied a rosebush in a nearby garden. Why was that creamy pink so impossible on the canvas? His sense of the day as perilous was not so much about other people's responses to his six canvases—of course he wanted them to like them—but about his own. In his small studio he had never been able to see the paintings, which he thought of as a single work, side by side. Last night, when they were finally on the wall, he could not bear to look but had turned away to help hang his friend Gio's lithographs.

If he had glanced up from the rosebush, he might have seen Zoe's plane circling Heathrow, waiting for permission to land.

She had taken an overnight flight from Chicago, where she lived with Rufus. He taught at a university and edited a journal, and she wrote poetry and worked with autistic children, most of whom had no use for language. On the plane she held her un-opened book and tried to figure out why Rufus wasn't sitting be-side her. Which of them had mentioned the expense, or the paper he was trying to write? She wasn't sure, but she added this trip to the list she had begun to keep of things they would once have done together and now, to save time or money, did separately. As the plane passed over Runnymede for the third time, she thought perhaps her days in America were numbered. She had lost her gift for slipping between the teeth of time.

Matthew, already at his office, was working on structuring a loan for a Greek shipping company. The sums were large, and exchange rates kept shifting unpredictably. He phoned a col-league in Berlin and planned a conference call to New York in the afternoon; everyone was wary. Looking up from today's fig-ures, he saw, across a few hundred yards of empty air, the leaded dome of St. Paul's Cathedral catching the morning sun. The day after they graduated from LSE, he and Benjamin had climbed up to the Golden Gallery beneath the dome and, looking south across the Thames, sworn a pact; they would make money for ten years and then do something useful: dig wells, fund small farms. If I weren't a coward, he thought now, I'd have quit two years ago. His girlfriend, Camille, had suggested they buy each other round-the-world tickets for Christmas.

After his walk with Lily, Duncan went to the primary school, where he worked as a teacher's assistant, painting with the children, reading them stories, settling disputes. Zoe made her way to Matthew's flat in Clerkenwell. Matthew continued to juggle figures; a German bank agreed to take on ten percent of the loan. The sun rolled up the sky; clouds—stratus, cumulus, cumulonimbus, altostratus—began to appear in the west. Duncan's fellow students bought a crate of rosé wine, two dozen bottles of sparkling water, wedges of Brie and Gouda, a big bowl of strawberries, and a smaller one of almonds. Duncan spent twenty pounds on perfectly blue cornflowers. Last year he had met Vanessa at the Columbia Street market when they both reached for a bunch of cornflowers. Six weeks ago they had agreed they were too busy to see each other.

When Zoe came into the degree show, her hair still damp from the shower, she sensed at once the presence of his paintings. Since she moved to the States, she had seen his work only occasionally, a sketch here, a small painting there. Now she was filled with trepidation. She wanted so badly for the paintings to be wonderful, for Duncan to have captured what he'd been working toward. First a drink. She poured herself a glass of rosé. Turning from the table, she caught sight of him across the room, standing beside a large leafy sculpture. How handsome he was with his dark hair tied back in a ponytail, his elegant black jacket over his white shirt.

"Zoe, you made it." His face glowed. He embraced her, careful not to spill her wine. They were still exclaiming—the flight was fine; she was so glad to be here—when Matthew arrived and hugged both of them. He had come straight from the office and was still in that hinterland between businessman and brother.

"So where are your paintings?" he said.

Duncan steeled himself. Wordless, he led the way to the wall where his work hung. He stopped in front of the first painting, Zoe on his left, Matthew on his right. Feeling them on either side, their eyes reaching toward the canvas, he was, at last, able to take in the crimson gashes, the soft greens and golds, the black lines which only he knew were swallows, darting.

It was Matthew who spoke first. "You painted the boy in the field."

"I wondered," Duncan said, "if you'd guess." He did not say—there was no need—that these paintings, titled I to VI, were the culmination and distillation of many, many canvases, many, many attempts.

Zoe, too, had known at once that this was Karel, or not exactly Karel but the essence of Karel, of what had happened that day in the field. She remembered kneeling beside him, calm in the face of his bloody legs, unaware that, through his closed eyelids, he saw the three of them.

"I wanted to make twelve," Duncan said. "A Stations of the Cross, like Agnes Martin or Barnett Newman, but the last one turned out to be the last." Gradually he could see the painting, see it whole. It works, he thought. I think it works.

"I love the blue," Matthew said as they moved on to II.

Evening sunlight, the particular gold of midsummer, poured through the high windows, mingling with the angled lights. When Duncan came to London to study art, Matthew had said, Show me the paintings you like. Together they had gone to galleries and museums. Standing in front of the canvases his brother deemed worthy, Matthew had struggled to learn how to look at abstract art; how to find the door into a painting where nothing was anything else.

They were still standing in front of III when, straight from the train, their parents arrived, Betsy flushed from the heat, worrying that they were late; Hal, his shirtsleeves neatly rolled, taking in the tall room and its occupants. More embraces, exclamations. How splendid that Zoe had come. What would they make of the paintings, Matthew thought, not knowing their true subject? "You have to begin at I," he said, leading the way.

"Is Esmeray here?" Betsy asked, searching the room.

"She's on flights to Sardinia this week. Look what she made me for graduation." Duncan held open his jacket to display the deep red lining.

"How elegant." Betsy gestured at the first painting. "This is beautiful."

"But a little menacing." Hal pointed to a different part of the painting. "Storm clouds are gathering."

"Let me get you some wine," Zoe said. Making her way through the crowd, she pondered again the mystery of their parents' reconciliation. Somehow they had got past her father's betrayal. Miranda, his younger daughter, often visited them at weekends. And yet, she thought, squeezing past a man in a dashiki, here she was still struggling to forgive Rufus for missing the poetry reading she'd given last autumn.

By the time she returned with two glasses of wine, they were back in front of III. She could see her parents straining to say the right thing while Matthew talked easily about the space of the painting, the brushwork, and Duncan stood, silently confronting the canvas. How cruel it was, this moment when the gap between one's secret imaginings and what one had made became public: an X-ray of one's mind.

"I thought you might be working on still lifes," Hal said. "Remember how you adored Morandi?"

"He's here," Duncan said, "though most people won't know it." He stepped back, trying to take in all six paintings, but there were too many people moving back and forth. V, he thought, was a little tentative, the gestures tangling awkwardly. He would come back tomorrow, first thing, to look at the paintings alone.

The sunlight dimmed and then, reflecting off the nearby buildings, flared. Ice cubes melted in minutes. People gently fanned themselves, or each other. Betsy and Hal moved on to look at the work of the other students. Duncan rejoined Matthew and Zoe in front of the last painting, VI, the one where chaos was let loose.

Separately and together, they remembered Karel, the boy in the field, who had on the day they found him not gone down to the underworld, who could see the swallows even when he closed his eyes, who had offered his understanding like a flower borne of sweetness, darkness, but which too many people had misunderstood. Two years ago Hugh Price had contacted each of them. While his parents were paying their summer visit to the Czech Republic, Karel, no longer afraid, had taken his own life. He had left a note: *No one is to blame.*

In the aftermath of the detective's call, Matthew and Zoe had each tried to phone Duncan. But Duncan was lying on the floor of his studio, with Lily beside him, gazing up at the ceiling, recalling that gray November afternoon when he had met Karel at the Cottage Hospital and walked beside him. He remembered the topaz-colored snail inching along the wall, the faint click of the bicycle wheels, the even fainter words, "Sometimes I wish you hadn't."

A few miles away Matthew, his call unanswered, had headed out into the narrow streets around his office, searching the buildings and the faces of passersby for clues: Why? Why? Why? Here was the site of the first hospital in London, here was where Henry VIII had kept his wardrobe, here was a woman, smiling secretly as she crossed the road. If only Karel had waited, he thought. Someone would have made him want to stay.

In Chicago, Zoe too had left the house; she had gone down to walk beside the endless lake. She remembered Karel, at the Salon, describing the river that separated him from the happy family—how he had longed and feared to cross it. I hope you're in the kingdom of reeds, she thought, with music and food and friends who need nothing from you. She threw a cowrie—her childhood collection still sat on her desk—into the wavy water.

Now, side by side, as the last of the evening light struck the wall, she and her brothers stood before Duncan's painting, ignoring the heat, their lukewarm drinks, the other people.

"His name is there," Duncan said quietly, pointing to the lower right corner of the canvas, a dark blue gesture slashed with black. "You can't see it, but I put his name in each painting."

"And then you painted it over," said Matthew. "Perfect."

Their parents returned. From one glance at their children,

they seemed to understand that speech was not needed. Betsy stood beside Zoe; Hal beside Matthew. Silently the five of them gave themselves over to Duncan's painting. Their attention, their devotion, began to draw that of others. Soon a small crowd gathered to gaze at the boy in the field.

ACKNOWLEDGMENTS

In 2008 the Metropolitan Museum held a retrospective of the works of Giorgio Morandi. His paintings emanated; I am grateful to have been in their presence.

My thanks to the pupil at Dalton School who, years ago, asked why the animals in my stories don't talk. Very belatedly, this is an attempt at an answer.

An article about the work of the painter Peter Sacks gave me certain crucial insights.

My dear friend Nancy Cartwright talked to me about philosophy.

On page 127, Zoe and Rufus discuss Ursula Le Guin's story "The Ones Who Walk Away from Omelas."

I am once again happily indebted to Amanda Urban, my agent, for helping this book to find a home and to Jennifer Barth, my editor, for giving it one. I am especially grateful to Jennifer for her devoted editing of this manuscript over many months; no subordinate clause was too trivial for her attention. My endless thanks to Jane Beirn for being such an eloquent ambassador for my work, and for many excellent reading recommendations. And thank you to all the other stellar people at HarperCollins—especially Jonathan Burnham, Amy Baker, and Becca Putman. Sarah Ried graciously answered my many questions. Joanne O'Neill gave the novel its beautiful cover.

I am grateful to my exemplary colleagues and students at the

Acknowledgments

Iowa Writers' Workshop, especially Lan Samantha Chang, Connie Brothers, and Sasha Khmelnik.

Four keen-eyed, opinionated readers gave very particular advice on the manuscript. David Musson offered comments and suggestions on every aspect of the story and the setting. My thanks for his wonderful accuracy and my apologies if I sometimes failed him. Susan Brison led me to understand certain key scenes in a new way. I am grateful to her insights into trauma and for her amazing book *Aftermath*. Eric Garnick entered into the arc of the narrative and made many helpful suggestions about the art and the lives of my characters. And Andrea Barrett read draft after draft, answered question after question, talked about these characters and their journeys as if they were our neighbors. I am so grateful to her for keeping me company and for rescuing me from many wrong turns.

ABOUT THE AUTHOR

MARGOT LIVESEY is the *New York Times* bestselling author of the novels *Mercury*, *The Flight of Gemma Hardy*, *The House on Fortune Street*, *Banishing Verona*, *Eva Moves the Furniture*, *The Missing World*, *Criminals*, and *Homework*. She has also published *The Hidden Machinery: Essays on Writing*. Her work has appeared in *The New Yorker*, *Vogue*, and the *Atlantic*, and she is the recipient of grants from both the National Endowment for the Arts and the Guggenheim Foundation. *The House on Fortune Street* won the L.L. Winship / PEN New England Award. Livesey was born in Scotland; she lives in the Boston area and is a professor of fiction at the Iowa Writers' Workshop.

ALSO BY MARGOT LIVESEY

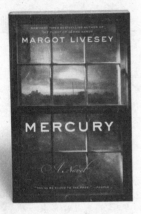

MERCURY
A Novel

"*Mercury* explores that thrilling, terrifying moment when grief turns blind, when passion becomes obsession. As always, Livesey tells her tale masterfully, with intelligence, tenderness and a shrewd understanding of all our mercurial human impulses."

—Lily King, author of *Writers & Lovers*

THE FLIGHT OF GEMMA HARDY
A Novel

"A suspenseful, curl-up-by-the-fire romance with a willfully determined protagonist who's worthy of her literary role model."

—*People*

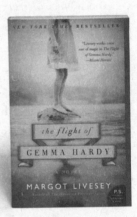

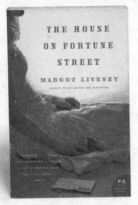

THE HOUSE ON FORTUNE STREET
A Novel

"Resonant, heartbreaking. . . . A spectacularly compassionate work, brimming with sharp insight into why we do the things we do, even when we know we shouldn't."

—*Miami Herald*